THE FRENCH FRAUD

JUSTINE FRENCH MYSTERIES

MYRTLE MORSE

BRITISH AUTHOR

Please note, this book is written in British English and
contains British spellings.

BOOKS IN THE SERIES

THE GREAT ESCAPE

The threatening letter pinned to the door of the pied-à-terre I was renting should have been my cue to pack my bags and go. For one, it was written in English, and for two, I knew that I hadn't lived in the small French town of Sellenoise long enough to ruffle the kind of feathers that needed ruffling if you wanted to be on the receiving end of a venomous note. *Just give me time*, I thought darkly. Trouble and I were in a complicated relationship with one another. I'd try to stay away from it, but inevitably, we always ended up getting back together.

But trouble turning up on my doorstep this quickly was a cause for concern.

I took the letter inside the grey stone cottage and did some nail biting. I knew who it was from. Both the threat and the cursive lettering made connections in my brain that caused a name to flash in bright, neon lights, reminding me of what I'd done to an unsuspecting, innocent woman.

Not that innocent, I silently amended, re-reading the letter and noting the vivid way in which my impending demise - which was apparently rapidly approaching - had been described. I also acknowledged that the letter could have been posted through my perfectly functional letterbox, instead of being slapped on the door like a wanted poster. Some people had a flair for the dramatic.

I sighed and tossed the letter from my ex-client into the wood burner, where it blackened and curled on the remnants of the logs that were still smouldering from last night's fire.

I'd never intended to cause any harm. At the time, I hadn't known that I'd made an error. That was actually the problem. I was *supposed* to know things like that.

I left the letter to become ash and walked into the kitchen to make myself some apple and cinnamon tea. A breeze blew through the window I'd opened prior to going out to the boulangerie to breathe some life into the dark cottage. The scent of woodsmoke, mushrooms, and damp soil was carried in on the wind, and I shut my eyes for a moment and listened to it whisper of autumn and a new start. I gazed out at the rolling green hills and trees that coated the landscape as far as the eye could see, scarlet and yellow leaves making it look like a forest aflame. For the first time in a long time, I felt something inside me move in response to my surroundings. It was a feeling that suggested this could be somewhere to stay for a while. It could be somewhere I might one day *belong*.

Maybe this time would be different.

I bit my lip when I remembered the letter. That was a definite blip in an otherwise blemish-free beginning. My ex-client was angry, but in my experience, people seldom did the things they threatened to do in writing. If everyone really meant what they said, or wrote, in anger, I'd be six-feet under several times over already. Still… it was strange that she'd managed to find me so quickly.

I'd already said sorry. I'd even sent her flowers. Some people needed an outlet for their rage. This letter was probably Hilda March's way of getting rid of the last of the bad feeling between us. It was a parting shot.

I poured boiling water from the kettle I'd brought to France with me over the sachet of dried apple, cinnamon, and hibiscus. I hadn't even done anything close to awful enough to justify this kind of reaction. I'd never claimed to know *everything.* Just… little bits. Not even the best of the best could see everything. At the end of the day, there was still an element of guesswork involved, and sometimes guesswork meant that certain things were glossed over.

Glossing over something as significant as the beloved pet I'd been employed to find having turned up his toes was apparently not considered an acceptable omission.

In my defence, the dog in question had been exceedingly elderly. After spending far too much time in his owner's company, I'd grown to understand why the old boy had thrown caution to the wind and decided to spend his last days running wild and engaging in some end of life antics that would make a nun blush. It was during one of these lively adventures with a toy poodle that the little terrier had keeled over. I was pretty certain that he'd died a happy dog after a long and very spoiled existence, but Mrs March had made it abundantly clear that I was supposed to have found her little terror *alive.* And I had promised that I would return him to her.

*Or had she said 'her little **terrier**'?* I mused with my tongue pressed into my cheek.

I'd never actually specified finding him *alive,* but bickering over my customer service promise hadn't seemed the right thing to do when I'd found Mr Finklesworth with all four legs in the air in the company of a very bemused poodle. I'd even returned my fee, in spite of delivering everything I'd promised when I'd taken on the case. The dog had been found, and my job had been completed.

If I'd been a private detective, that sort of thing would probably have been accepted with good grace and no hard feelings. I'd have collected my cheque without any trouble.

It was different when you were a psychic.

Not a real one. I was close to certain that they didn't exist.

I'd never planned to become the kind of person who claims to be something that they're not. It had happened accidentally when I'd found myself in a difficult situation with the police. There'd been no reasonable explanation for me knowing the things I'd known about a case that they'd been investigating. Or rather - no explanation that they would have reasonably believed.

Which was why I'd come up with something unbelievable.

I breathed in the spicy scent of cinnamon mixed with the sweetness of the apple, warming my hands on my favourite cup, which featured a sassy, bright pink cat with a speech bubble that reminded me to 'Have a Purrfect Day!' It was amazing how the human psyche would rather accept something that was unexplainable and impossible to prove, as opposed to an actual reasonable explanation - which was merely vastly complicated to explain and prove. That was why I'd told the police that I was psychic, and I'd foolishly imagined that it would be the end of it.

It had been the end of it... until the press had asked the police how they'd cracked the case and one of the dimmer officers had shared that they'd had the help of a psychic investigator. Some of the journalists had been no slouches themselves when it came to investigating. It hadn't been long before the bright sparks had figured out my name, found a photo of me, and had slapped both on newspaper front pages, accompanied by the headline: 'Psychic Solves Robbery!'

I'd bitten my tongue very hard when I'd seen that. Prior

to the unwanted feature, I'd been working as a therapist, using my very un-magical powers of observation to help people fix their life problems. Paying the bills had not been easy every month, but I was the sort of person who enjoyed making other people happy. I was a people pleaser, and that was more important than being rich and - what most people might consider - successful.

At least... that was what I'd told myself before I'd started making money.

Really good money.

I took a sip of my tea and shut the window on the cold morning air, returning to the little sitting room and plonking myself down on a rug-covered settee that sagged with age. When the papers had gone wild over the little white lie I'd told to get myself out of a hard to explain situation, I'd thought it would be the kind of thing everyone forgot about in a week. Surely no one really believed in psychic powers?

It had only been when my aunt had called me and asked if I knew what her husband was really up to when he went out to play golf on Friday afternoons - because she'd noticed strange stains on the knees of his golfing trousers - that I'd realised there were people who'd taken the tabloids seriously. When I'd opened my email inbox and discovered hundreds of enquiries from people asking me to solve mysteries they believed were unsolvable, I'd been forced to accept that my aunt wasn't the only believer.

Even more astonishingly, most of the people had offered sizeable rewards if I could use my 'powers' to help solve their problems.

I glanced up when the daylight that illuminated the little sitting room was blocked out by a shadow. For the briefest of moments, alarm spiked through me. Thoughts of black-cloaked assassins and mad axe men jumped into my head. The threatening letter must have got under my skin after all.

The shadow turned out to be Pierre's round, reddish face, peering in at me. His cheeks were like two apples, and joy danced in his eyes when he wiggled his fingers in greeting. I waved back, knowing I would be automatically smiling in return, like we were best friends, instead of just landlord and renter.

Sometimes, the people pleaser thing was a pain. It meant everyone assumed you were their friend, even when you would rather run a mile, jump a stile, and eat a country pancake than have dinner *chez* Pierre's. He had a face friendlier than Father Christmas, which made the fact that he was a total pervert even more unsettling. I'd like to be able to say that checking the walls of the terraced property I was renting from him for peepholes wasn't something I'd done out of a hard-learned habit, but these days, I travelled carrying a caulk gun and a tube full of filler. Landlords should be grateful to me for repairing their compromised walls and empty-eyed paintings.

I breathed a silent sigh of relief when Pierre was distracted by an attractive brunette carrying a crusty baguette from the popular local boulangerie... and then nearly inhaled my tea when my neighbour on the other side whacked him around the head with yesterday's baguette. I grinned when she yelled at him for being a lech. Eloise was the saving grace of my current living situation. She kept Pierre under control - often with whatever she was holding in her hand at the time - and, remarkably, he respected her for it. Even though the pair fought like cats in a bag, I knew there was more to their relationship than just war.

I also knew that some things were better left unsaid.

Which was why I should never have said to all of those people who'd offered enough money to pay my rent for an entire month with their rewards: 'Yes, I can definitely solve your mysteries. And, yes... of course I'm a real psychic!'

At first, it had just seemed like a neat marketing gimmick. I loved solving people's problems, and having scores of people with problems that needed solving had made me as happy as a dog in a sausage factory. If my unique selling point was calling myself a psychic, then so be it. The route to solving the problem didn't matter, so long as the problem ended up solved.

I'd never stopped to think what my response would have been if someone had said something like that to me in one of my genuine therapy sessions. It was just like the old joke about hairdressers being able to cut everyone's hair but their own - I was a therapist who hadn't been able to see when she would have benefitted from taking her own advice.

Advice like... not building a career based on a lie whilst telling oneself it was all done with good intentions. Because no matter how good your intentions are, if you're not what you claim to be, one day, the sky will fall on your head.

I placed my empty cup down and rubbed the space between my eyebrows. The sky may not be falling on my head, but I definitely felt a headache brewing. Perhaps it was the change of season, or maybe there was a storm on the horizon. I considered the pink pom-pom slippers in front of the sofa, before turning towards the pink trainers I'd left by the entrance to the sitting room. Some people relaxed by sitting at home and turning on the TV, or curling up with a good book. I enjoyed reading and crafting, but the only way for me to really relax was to get outside and as far away from other people as possible to calm the buzzing in my mind. It was an occupational hazard of being a therapist. If there were other people involved - even in books or on television - I would be unravelling their thoughts and actions, searching for the meaning behind it all.

It was one of the reasons why I'd chosen the French

region of Creuse for this extended holiday. Out here, isolation was pretty easy to come by.

I finally decided on the fuchsia wellies that had been gifted to me by Annabelle, my best friend back home in England, and I stepped outside the cottage. There was a chill in the air that whipped down the street, pushing fallen leaves with it in a lively whirlwind. It implied there could be a change in the weather on the way. For now though, the sun was shining in a blue sky dotted with cotton ball clouds, and I felt the heart of the forest calling my name. Five minutes later, I was lost beneath tall birch trees with the thick River Sellen a few metres to the left of the path and nothing but woods and hills to the right. It was simple to avoid people out here.

A frown danced on my forehead for a moment when I considered that last thought. Understanding people was my livelihood, my passion, and yet... sometimes, I needed a break from people and their problems. When it came to running away from problems, this little French town was the best place for it.

I smiled as I stepped over a clump of bright yellow mushrooms and continued on my lonely way along the river. *If only my mother could have seen where I am now!* I thought, remembering the formidable lady with fondness. Growing up, I'd longed to be like her with her poker straight, jet black hair and eyes like bright coals that warned you of serious consequences if you did something that displeased her. Formidable was the only word to describe the woman who had moved countries on her own with a small child in tow and proceeded to not only start her own restaurant, but quickly gain renown for her traditional French cooking that had brought strangers from far and wide to the little village of Forest Acre. I'd wanted to be just like her - made of steel and stone and impossible for the world to knock down.

Instead, I'd been blonde and chubby. Soft and squishy in every sense with a personality that was sent into a frenzy of inner worry whenever someone refused the slice of cake or cup of tea I'd offered them - because I was certain it meant they must *hate* me.

As the years had become decades, I'd accepted that I was never going to be someone like my mother - not least because I preferred cake to savoury stews - but I had managed to get a handle on my worrying. I'd realised that the reason I was concerned about what people thought and felt was because I usually knew exactly what they were thinking and feeling. And what's more, when I'd finally stopped worrying about what they were thinking about *me* and moved my focus back to *them*, I'd found I could work out a whole lot more than simply what they were thinking and feeling.

That was how I'd discovered I'd inherited one of my mother's gifts after all.

It had happened when she'd been hiring a new chef. A man with a reputation so fantastic it would surely have brought people down from London to eat at her restaurant had applied for the job. I'd watched the entire interview process in awe. He'd made the most marvellous *magret de canard à l'orange* and had finished the meal with a triple chocolate mouse that had nearly brought tears to my eyes when I'd tasted it. Even though the chef had already made a name for himself, he'd explained that he was such a huge admirer of my mother and her secret recipes that he wanted to stay in Forest Acre and train in her way of doing things. It was an incredible compliment to receive from such an accomplished chef.

She hadn't given him the job.

When she'd been instructing her new chef on how to

correctly make custard, I'd asked her why she'd gone with a complete novice instead of the culinary genius.

It was the only time she'd ever looked disappointed in me.

"If you don't know why I overlooked the other chef, then I am worried that the world will not be kind to you, *mon petit chou*." She'd watched me expectantly, and I'd been forced to think very carefully about the answer my mother was looking for.

"He had debts," I'd said after a long pause.

"And how do you know that?"

I'd told her about the borrowed shirt he'd worn to the interview that was one size too big for him. There'd been sap stains around the button hole from when it had been worn to a wedding before being loaned out to help a friend land a job. There'd also been tan lines where he'd once worn a watch and a ring, but they'd been removed and presumably sold to make ends meet.

"He could have been through a bad divorce, which resulted in him losing weight and selling things that reminded him of his ex-wife. How do you know he had unpaid debts?" she'd repeated, and I'd been forced to think again... because I'd been certain that I was on the right track.

"He had... bruises on his chest. They were only visible when he leaned forwards. There was a mark on his ear, too. Like someone tattooed him with one of those at home kits. It said: DNP. That could have been initials, but someone brave enough to have a tattoo openly displaying initials of someone they care about has usually got more than one tattoo in a visible place. It's not a first tattoo... and it wasn't done very well, which indicates that either the person doing it didn't have much experience with a tattoo gun, or he didn't want to get a tattoo and struggled... or both. DNP could be Did Not Pay or Debt Not Paid. In combination with the bruises designed to be in places that wouldn't stop him from getting a job, and thus being able to pay off his debts, it equals money problems, rather than domestic issues. Plus, the tan line from the ring wasn't on his ring finger."

"I'd have settled for the ring hadn't been on his ring finger," my mother had told me, but in spite of her cool words, she'd been impressed. I thought I may have even seen more than she had that day.

"But he was still a good chef. Everyone has problems. Having a job here could have helped him to pay off what he owed," I'd said when the warm glow of being right had faded a little.

My mother had levelled another knowing look at me. "There's a difference between having debts and letting debts have you. You can help those who want to be helped, but you've already told me that this man didn't suffer a divorce and likely has some very bad people on his tail. Did you see a good reason for him to have ended up in so much trouble?"

I'd considered again and had shaken my head.

My mother had nodded, satisfied. "Neither did I. And that is the most important observation of all. Ask yourself this: if he'd already lied to us about the reason why he wanted to work here, and there was no sign of any reason why he could justifiably be in so much debt, do you think he would have been an honest employee and worked hard to pay off those debts, if I'd given him a chance?"

"I think he'd have told more lies and tried to get more money... but not to pay off his debts," I'd replied, feeling it was true, but not quite understanding how I knew these things. All I'd been certain of was that it certainly wasn't magic - just a talent for seeing things that other people missed, or didn't know how to look for.

"Now you understand," was all my mother had said, before returning to teaching the chef she'd hired instead. That man had stayed with her even when she'd become too

11

unwell to handle the business. In the end, he'd taken over the restaurant, lovingly reproducing her dishes for diners who still travelled from miles around to visit a restaurant with a reservation list that was full for months in the future. The chef who hadn't even been able to make a proper custard had been a much better choice than the man who'd made chocolate mousse good enough to make me cry.

It wasn't long after I'd discovered the talent my mother had passed on to me that I'd also realised where we diverged from one another. I'd stopped worrying about what people thought about me, but I'd started worrying about what they thought of themselves and others. My mother had used her abilities to make excellent business decisions and read everything she needed to know from a person as soon as she met them, targeting weak points and using her knowledge to convince people to give her anything she needed. I'd wanted to use the same skill to help people live happy lives and understand things about themselves that they couldn't see, but I could... and I could tell them not only what they were feeling, and why, but also how they could change it.

I was never going to be called formidable the way my mother had been described to me in voices filled with reverence. On the contrary, I was the warm to her cold, and the wibbly-wobbly to her unyielding strength. People liked to tell me things because I wasn't a threat, and in my warm and fuzzy way, I had always been sure that I was putting a little bit of *good* back into the world.

Until I'd got carried away.

I kicked the spiky casing of a chestnut out of my path when I turned right at the fork and left the river behind me. *One mistake doesn't make you a bad person. Think of all the people you did help!* I thought, trying to convince myself it wasn't that bad. Prior to the Mr Finklesworth fiasco, I had helped people solve their mysteries and problems with my not so psychic abilities. Sure, they'd all *believed* I'd done it using a magical gift, but everyone had been happy with the results.

No one wants to live a lie forever - no matter how many good intentions it was originally told with. That was why I'd uprooted everything and announced I was travelling the world. Technically, that had been another white lie. I'd only ever intended to find somewhere in France to wait out any storms back home and was not at all keen on actually seeing the world. There were way too many people in it, and I was supposed to be taking a break from people.

That was why I'd picked France.

My mother had always told me that the French were slow to warm up to strangers. Even though I spoke fluent French, I knew it came with an accent that had made my mother's life hard whenever she'd moved away from Paris. No one was going to be queuing up to be my best friend. Beyond a polite 'bonjour' and everything that was necessary for me to make transactions, so far, I'd been treated with the usual mistrust extended to any stranger who appeared in a remote town in the middle of rural nowhere.

And that suited me just fine.

I huffed and puffed my way up one hill and several others after that. As well as avoiding people, I should probably start avoiding the sweeter things in life. It was going to be tough when I'd chosen a town with a really lovely patisserie in the town square. One of the best things about France was the food. I'd been taught that from a very young age.

A brown bird made a squawking sound of surprise and flew up out of a bush to the left of the trail I was walking along. I stepped off the not-so beaten track, deciding to do some exploring. In these parts, the bird was lucky I wasn't a hunter, or it would have been plucked and plated by dinner-time. At this time of year, it was probably unwise to be walking through the forest in anything other than colours bright enough to stop traffic. I glanced down at the pink rain jacket I'd put on to keep the wind chill out. I doubted deer dressed like this.

My thoughts about hunters made me stop and listen, but no sound beyond the wind hissing through the trees reached my ears. There wasn't even the distant rush of cars. No one had built roads anywhere close to this part of the forest, because there wasn't anywhere for the roads to lead to. I was miles away from civilisation in the middle of nowhere, walking beneath trees that I was sure hadn't witnessed more than a handful of humans passing beneath their boughs in their lifetime. It was hard to find places like this... places that felt forgotten.

It made discovering a body with an axe in its back even more shocking.

2

A SURPRISE WITNESS

"**F**luff on a stick!" I muttered, my eyes as wide as dinner plates. "Excuse me, monsieur, are you okay?" I tried in French, before wanting to slap my own cheek for being an idiot. It was pretty obvious that the man I'd just found in the middle of the forest was beyond answering stupid questions. He was beyond doing anything useful at all.

Because he was dead.

I did some rapid blinking and took several deep breaths, before remembering you were supposed to release the first breath before you took the next one. I flapped my hands around my face, like a demented ostrich. Everyone dealt differently with death. I'd seen firsthand the many and varying reactions people had to someone leaving the mortal coil, but my current reaction was surprising even me.

"It's because it's a total surprise... and not a good one!" I argued out loud with a brain that I knew was judging me and whispering that my mother certainly wouldn't have seen a corpse and *flapped*. "Mostly because there'd have been a semi-decent chance that she'd been the one *responsible* for a person ending up like this," I muttered.

Strangely, being annoyed helped me to calm down and get a grip on the worrywart side of me, who'd temporarily escaped the box I'd locked her up in years ago. I took a few moments to pull myself together, before I looked at the body again with a clearer mind. There was nothing I could do to help immediately. The time for that had long passed. If the lack of breathing hadn't been hint enough that there was no life in the man lying on the forest floor, the bloodstained wounds and the axe embedded in his back definitely sealed the deal.

I bent down and tilted my head, noting the unnatural mottling of the skin on his face, which featured shades of purple and green that indicated this incident hadn't occurred five minutes ago. The body had been in the forest for a while. I was no forensic expert, but the corpse was somewhere on the scale between rigour-mortis setting in and starting to mulch down into a skeleton.

Yup… that really narrowed it down.

Someone who was psychic was supposed to be able to touch a hand to their temple or go into a mystical trance and immediately know the answer to questions like: 'How long has this body been in the woods?' As I wasn't actually psychic, or a scientist, I had to work it out based on other factors, and then pretend I knew the answers because I was psychic.

"You don't have to work it out. You're not doing that anymore!" I said out loud, reminding myself that this was supposed to be a fresh start, a new page, an un-popped pack of Pringles. There would be no visions, no insights, and definitely no claims of being anything other than an ordinary therapist, who just wanted to help people live happier lives. I glanced back at the body. A hundred observations ran through my head in a split second.

Fluff and bother.

Now I knew that the axe in his back was not the kind you bought in a general hardware store. It was old... ancient, probably. It looked worn with age and the metal had degraded in places. And yet... the bloodstained half of the edge that was visible without touching the body had been sharpened and shone with care and smoothness. The axe had been ready for use, perhaps honed by a killer who'd planned their murderous act well in advance. There were mush-rooms, too... picked and scattered around the body. There was one on top of the dead man's sleeve, which told me that they'd been added after he'd expired. Someone had left mushrooms here for a reason.

"Nope. *Non*. This is a job for the police," I said, tearing my eyes away from the distressing scene and pulling out my mobile phone.

Oh.

Right.

I'd forgotten that the downside of being out in the middle of nowhere was that there was a distinct absence of the usual conveniences of modern civilisation, like mobile phone masts. I had zero signal.

What did you expect in a place where you're considered fancy if you have mains drainage? I thought blithely, as I looked around for the nearest hill to climb and realised I was already up pretty high. The good old 'climb a hill and wave your phone around' strategy probably wouldn't work here after all. *What about climbing a tree?* Even though the thought was utterly ridiculous - firstly, because there was no way I was going to take up tree climbing at the getting dangerously close to a 'mature adult' age of thirty-four, and secondly, because if I fell out of the tree and plummeted to the ground, I'd end up in a worse state than when I'd started... and still have no phone signal.

"Huh..." I muttered when I noticed something up in a tree that definitely seemed strange. My previous deduction that I was in a part of the forest where nobody came was really taking a beating. You didn't put a CCTV camera in a place that no one visited.

It was pretty strange to have CCTV in the middle of even a relatively crowded forest, but its presence here was... weird. I stuck my hands on my hips, wondering what type it was. Probably not the kind that was watched like a hawk from a security office, or this body wouldn't have been lying out here for so long - not unless the person watching was the one responsible and had set up a camera for some twisted enjoyment... but I knew that wasn't right. There was a dusty, green film of lichen that covered the camera which let me know it had been here far longer than the new addition to the little clearing. As I squinted at it, I also noted the absence of any visible wires or power source.

The camera was fake, but the question remained the same... why was there something that looked like a CCTV camera out in the middle of nowhere? If I were the police, it would be one of the first questions I'd be asking.

But I wasn't the police... so it was really none of my business.

I made a small sound of frustration. It was so hard to take a holiday. Especially when you knew there was a violent killer on the loose.

A killer who might regularly hang around in the forest near to where they'd murdered their last victim.

A twig snapped and I squeaked in alarm.

The ominous rustling of a nearby bush did nothing to settle my nerves.

Someone was toying with me.

My pulse pumped out a rhythm in my ears, and my fingers clenched and unclenched on palms that had become sweaty in an instant - another not so useful talent of mine. My blue eyes flicked over to the axe embedded in the corpse - the only weapon in the vicinity that could possibly help me to defend myself against... well... against a mad axe murderer. *You can't use it! It's destruction of evidence at a crime scene!* the voice in my head screamed, panicking at the idea of doing something wrong, something impulsive, even though it could save my life.

I shut my eyes. Who was I kidding? Even if I did dash over and pull out that axe, I wouldn't be able to use it. I was a cushion collector, a cake eater, and a shoulder to cry on... not a fearsome warrior woman who could wield a weapon. I'd probably end up cutting off my own toes and still have to face whatever it was that was stalking me in this frightening forest.

Running probably wouldn't go too well for me either. Taking up jogging was one of those things I liked to think about and follow up with a hot chocolate to congratulate myself for having had such a healthy thought. No running actually took place, and now probably wasn't the time to start something I already knew was unlikely to be a new and surprising skill.

I was still standing around in my opposite-of-camouflage jacket when the sound of something running towards me at speed came from behind. I turned to face whatever monster it was that lurked in this forest.

But no mad axe murderer materialised.

Woof!

I lowered my gaze and met the golden eyes of a ginger and white dog. His tail waved back and forth and he tilted his head as he took me in, seeming to ask if I was a friend or a foe.

"Are you lost?" I asked him, before asking the same in French… as if he'd understand me better that way. It was official. I was losing the plot.

"It looks like we're going to have to do this the old fashioned way," I muttered, suddenly feeling a lot better now that the dog was present than when it had just been me having a conversation with a corpse.

I took one final look at the body in the clearing before turning back towards the town, which lay many miles away. "Are you coming?" I asked the dog, wondering if he lived out here, and if his owner was nearby. The lack of collar and the way his ribs were showing through his ginger coat hinted that he wasn't exactly living a life of luxury. Nor was he a wild dog, I judged from the manner in which his eyes watched me with both hope and fear.

He hesitated a while longer on the edge of a thick clump of trees. Then, he took one step towards me, and another, before he stopped. That was apparently as far as he would go.

I exhaled slowly, keeping my eyes on the dog whilst I considered the situation. I didn't have a lead or anything I could use to get the dog to come with me, and I doubted it was going to let me catch it either. "I'll look for you again when I've reported this," I promised my newest acquaintance, who sat down and scratched his ear in response. My heart was already breaking at the thought of an animal being abandoned out here.

I was a cat person through and through.

My mother had never liked dogs, claiming they slobbered over everything, but she'd had a grudging respect for cats. The restaurant had meant no pets, but that hadn't stopped the local strays from fishing in our bins, and I'd befriended as many of them as I could.

Dogs remained an unknown quantity that I generally treated with care and distance, and it just so happened that this dog felt the exact same way about humans.

"Good day to you, monsieur dog," I said, walking back towards the trail, still trying to wrap my head around the surreal situation I'd stumbled upon during what was supposed to have been a quiet walk in the forest to forget about past and present problems - like the one that had been pinned to my front door.

When I reached the official-ish trail, I looked back over my shoulder.

The dog was following me.

"Nice to know I'm better company than a body," I said as a horrible thought occurred to me. Did the dog belong to the man I'd found with the axe in his back? Had it been out here for days, waiting for someone to find its owner?

I dismissed the thought as soon as I had it. There'd been no dog fur anywhere on the corpse's clothing, and my mother had always been very careful to warn me about how pet hair got everywhere, and you could never, ever get rid of it. It had been one of the many reasons she'd cited to explain why we couldn't get a pet. This dog was every bit as alone as I was in this empty part of the world. "But at least we're not lost," I said aloud when I heard panting off to my left and knew he'd caught up.

The trail was winding and had many forks that led off in unknown directions with unknown destinations, but I never needed to worry about losing my way, even when the sound of the river echoed around the valley, seeming to come from every direction at once. Noticing things had its advantages when it came to navigating an area that no satellite navigation covered. I remembered the sycamore with the old bird's nest sitting in its branches and I recognised the stump with gelatinous mushrooms, which had been off to the left of the trail I had walked down. Getting lost was something that just didn't happen to me, which was lucky, because this was no time to be losing my bearings in a forest.

I had a murder to report.

3

CROISSANTS AND CRIME

The municipal police station looked closed.

When I tested the dark blue door by giving it a good tug, the only result was a few extra paint flakes joining the large number already accumulating on the concrete by the entrance. The door was locked.

I glanced up at the giant clock face on the side of the church spire and noted that it was past midday... and therefore probably lunchtime. So much for the emergency services never stopping.

I gave up on the door and walked over to the window, cleaning it with my sleeve, so that I could get a good look inside. Calling the emergency number was next on my to do list if this failed, but the lack of signal thing was not exclusive to the forest. It was a common feature in town, too. I'd already found that out to my cost and had only managed to get a single bar when I'd climbed right to the top of the view point. It was a climb I'd rather not do again after the miles I'd already covered today.

Especially when the people the number would put me in

contact with were only a few metres away, eating croissants with ham and cheese.

I banged on the glass and the two men turned around.

"We're closed!" one of them mouthed, pointing at his watch to make sure I got the message.

"There's been a murder!" I shouted back, but the local policeman pointed to his ear and indicated that he couldn't hear a word I was saying through the double glazing. Or - more likely - he'd immediately switched off, because I was a stranger and he wasn't keen on my big city accent.

"A... murder..." I repeated extra slowly for their benefit. Then, I did something inexplicable that I would agonise over later. Something that in no way added to my credibility in the eyes of this particular arm of the law.

I mimed chopping an axe and then grabbed my own throat, pretending to meet the kind of dramatic end that would feature on YouTube lists titled: 'Worst Cinematic Deaths Ever'. It wasn't surprising that the policemen exchanged a nervous look... as if I were far more suspicious than the murder I was here to report.

When the policeman on the left put down his croissant and walked out of the room and unlocked the front door, I decided it might have been worth it.

"Is there a problem?" he asked, his fingers twitching, as if he was already considering taking action against the unstable woman who'd just turned up at lunchtime - showing ignorance that some things are sacred - and had then acted alarmingly outside of the window. "The dog pound is full. You will have to deal with him yourself. I'm sorry," he said, his dark eyes apologetic. "This is not England," he added. "People are sometimes cruel to their animals here."

"There are people like that in every country," I informed him sadly, looking back at the dog, whose golden eyes were still watching my every move while he continued to make up his mind about the woman in pink that he'd met in the forest. "He was hanging around nearby when I found the body, but I don't think the dead man was his owner. There was no hair on his clothes," I said, not thinking about the words that were coming out of my mouth.

I was probably still suffering some kind of shock from coming face to face with a body.

It wasn't the first one I'd ever seen but it was the first unexpected one. That was the problem with being able to figure things out from various visible signs... when something did manage to surprise you, it really threw you off balance.

"I'm not unstable and in need of assistance, I'm just upset due to what I found in the forest," I said, reading the police agent's inner thoughts from his expression and the way his hands were now twitching towards his radio - which presumably connected to something that mobile phones couldn't.

The look of astonishment that crossed his face would have been amusing, if I hadn't seen it a thousand times before. People fell into two camps when you told them what they were thinking. They were either amazed, or very alarmed.

This man was edging towards the latter.

"You're saying... you found a body in the forest?" he asked hesitantly, still watching me in case I suddenly screamed in his face or started pulling balloon animals out from beneath my t-shirt.

"That's exactly what I'm saying. I would have called the emergency number immediately, but..." I waved my useless mobile phone at him. "...I had to walk back to report it."

"You should have that dog on a lead. People around here aren't keen on dogs running loose when they have their livestock to worry about," he told me, rubbing his clean-shaven chin and looking at the dog with thoughtful dark eyes.

I noticed the tattoo on his arm, written in Elvish, and wondered what it said, beyond telling everyone that he had a passing familiarity with Tolkien's great work. I wondered if he knew the books or the films.

"I think we've got a rope. No collar, but if we tie a loop in the rope and slip it over his head, it's surely better than nothing," he continued.

"Shouldn't someone go and investigate the body I found? I don't want to say too much, in case I'm wrong..." (I wasn't wrong.) "...but, it looked like there was foul play involved. I mean, I don't think it's possible to stab yourself in the back with an axe. Especially not multiple times. I'm not sure why anyone would want to do that to themselves, either."

"I can't imagine anyone doing that," the policeman agreed, continuing to rub his chin and look thoughtful - but not concerned or ready to spring into action.

I looked at him and he looked back, both of us aware that there was some kind of misunderstanding going on here, but neither of us knowing what it was.

"Let's get that rope!" he said, brightening at the idea and trotting back inside the municipal police station.

I exchanged a look with the dog, who'd decided to edge close enough to sit by my legs. I tentatively reached out a hand and received a polite sniff in response.

"Got it!" the policeman said, returning holding a small pile of climbing rope. He found the end and then expertly tied a knot that wouldn't tighten, even when pulled. At first, he dangled it in front of the dog, but his tail went between his legs and he backed away. With an apologetic look, he passed the rope to me.

I tilted my head at the dog, expecting him to have the same reaction when I took a couple of steps towards him with the rope outstretched. It was one thing to follow a human out of the woods in the hopes of getting some food, but quite another to actually trust someone. When the dog just kept looking at me and didn't even flinch when I slipped the loop over his head, I thought I understood. He'd undoubtedly had at least one bad experience with a person in the past. He hadn't lived in the forest all his life. Someone had put him there, but he was a dog, not a wild animal. And he needed someone to look after him.

"This is great! I thought I would be spending my whole afternoon catching a stray dog," the policeman said, smiling a smile so bright that it made me wonder what brand of toothpaste he used and whether it would work the same magic on me.

"But… there's a body. A death. A probable murder," I said, wondering if my French was rustier than I'd realised.

The man I was talking to nodded in understanding. "You have told me this already. We will wait for the chief of police, Monsieur Duval, to finish his lunch, and then we will investigate. Can you show me where it was on a map?"

"I… no, probably not. I'd left the path to go exploring," I confessed.

The policeman sucked air through his spectacular teeth. "Then, it will probably take a long time for us to locate the body, before it can be verified and further help requested. The forest is very big. It is easy for someone to get lost and get into trouble where no help will come."

"Isn't that all the more reason for us to go and find the body again right now? Lunch can wait!" Those were not words that usually came out of my mouth. "Why is this not being treated as an emergency?"

The municipal police agent did a fantastic approximation of the gallic shrug. "It's a big forest… it would have been more likely that the animals would have found him before any other human, had you not stumbled upon this scene. And even with you saying you saw something earlier... we will see if we find it again. Things go missing out in the woods all the time. We live in a remote part of the country." He gazed off towards the dark green and reddish-gold hues of the forest, which was visible between a gap in buildings in the town square.

"I have a feeling that at least one other person probably knows this area of the forest. There was a security camera up in a tree, and I can't point out on a map where I was, but I can show you myself," I said, kind of wishing I'd just started by listing everything I'd observed about the scene of the crime, but I knew what that sort of thing led to, didn't I? It led to questions, and then - inevitably - trouble. I was treading carefully, even if treading carefully meant coming across like the town's new resident idiot as I struggled to not say too much... but to also say enough to convince this man and his croissant-crunching superior that I was telling the truth.

Whilst not being personally guilty of any crime.

So far, I'd rate my performance a solid one out of ten. Maybe even less, because the man I was talking to was looking less happy-go-lucky and more suspicious by the second.

"You're new here, aren't you?" he asked, even though we both knew he was well aware that I was.

Nobody slipped silently into a place like this. If there was a stranger in town, it would be the news of the week, quite possibly the month, and if the year was a particularly slow one...

"It takes locals their whole lives to navigate the parts of the forest where there are no pathways. Most use maps that have been passed down through generations, but even then..." He let out a whistle and shook his head. "People around here view finding your way through the forest as an art - like magic. I think you are very lucky to even be standing here in front of me, if you truly left the path. I do not think you will be able to return to this place. This is not like walking through Hyde Park in London," he finished, proudly showing off his knowledge of England.

"I'm a quick learner," I replied, managing a smile that usually had people desperate to tell me their biggest worries. I had one of those faces that made others want to share things. "I'm Justine French," I added, when the police agent continued to look at me like I was a puzzle comprised solely of slightly varying hues of pink - and therefore nearly impossible to put together.

"Marius Bisset," he replied, nodding politely at me, his dark eyes still watchful. I did my best to keep a frown from creasing my forehead. I was not used to people thinking that I was complicated.

I opened my mouth to try to start all over again and do a better job of explaining how I'd come to find the body, why I thought it was more urgent than lunch, and how I knew I'd be able to find it again, but the door to the police station opened and a grey-haired man with crumbs in his moustache walked out. He pressed both hands into his lower back and pushed his paunch forwards, making the sort of groan those familiar with working eight hour days behind a desk would recognise. "Why is she still here?" he said, addressing Marius and completely ignoring me.

"I'm still here because there is still a body out in the forest, waiting for someone to find out who put it there," I told him.

He stared at me as if I'd broken some unwritten code by understanding every word that had come out of his mouth and answering him back.

"She says she can take us to the location. It's quite far

from the path, apparently," Marius helpfully contributed, but he didn't bother to conceal his skepticism.

"I'll bet you a free lunch on me that I can find it without getting lost," I muttered, starting to let my frustration get the better of me.

Something that looked a lot like amusement flashed in Marius' dark eyes, but his boss remained unimpressed.

The chief of police's moustache bristled. "Even people who've lived here their whole lives get lost for days in that forest. There's something strange about the trees. You don't have a hope of finding…"

"Watch me!" I interrupted, losing patience with the two men, who'd rather stand around talking than actually take any action.

"It's a serious offence to waste police time! You could be charged with a crime," the croissant-eater called after me.

I turned around and looked at him. "It's a long walk. I'm only doing it one more time today, and then I have an appointment with *The Vicar of Dibley* and a tin of biscuits. Follow me, or you'll be wasting far more of your own time searching the forest when someone in town reports a missing person."

There. I could be tough talking when I needed to be. Most people needed warm and fuzzy commiseration and empathy to iron themselves out, but others needed a verbal smack around the head with a big stick.

"Who's the vicar of Dibley?" the grey-haired man asked, his eyebrows knitting together as the plot seemed to thicken for him.

"It's a television… never mind," I said, not entirely surprised that comedy hadn't reached France yet.

"How do you know that someone will report this person missing from our town?" Marius asked, surprising me with a question that showed he was paying attention. Too much attention, if truth be told.

I weighed up the lie against the truth and decided to land somewhere in-between. I needed to remember that I wasn't doing anything wrong. I just wanted to stay out of trouble. Keep my nose clean. Not miss out on some cosy me-time when the municipal police decided to throw me in their jail because they thought I knew too much without a good explanation as to why.

"Well... there aren't any other towns within a twenty minute drive, are there? It's logical that he came from here." I tried my best to look jolly and innocuous, resisting the urge to add: Also, there was a badge on the edge of his lapel with the town's crest on it bearing the initials: S.M.C. (Sellenoise Municipal Council). That was the sort of thing I knew a casual observer was not supposed to have noticed. In any case, it did no harm to keep it from them because they would be seeing it for themselves very soon.

Or at least - they would be, if we could stop standing around shooting the breeze and get inside the forest before nightfall, when even my powers of observation might let me down when it came to finding the way.

"Do we need to pack some sandwiches for the trip, or can we start walking?" I smiled sweetly, knowing it was very hard for people to work out when I was being sarcastic, even when I really wished they'd know.

"This isn't a picnic!" Monsieur Duval snapped, immediately marching off in the direction of the forest. "Come on!" he shouted back, as if I were the one who'd been dragging my heels whilst digesting my lunch.

Marius popped in and out of the police station, coming out with a big bag that he slung over his shoulders. "We'd better catch up to him, or we'll be looking for a body *and* a badly orientated, bad-tempered chief of police."

"I know which one I'd prefer to find," I said without thinking.

Marius shot me another of those almost amused looks. "I got this for your dog," he said, pulling out a large, cured sausage. "Sometimes we get given gifts by people in town," he said, as if I'd already asked him for an explanation as to why the local police station kept sausages lying around the place.

The dog certainly didn't ask any questions when I passed him the sausage, and he made remarkably short work of it. It wasn't the healthiest choice for a dog's dinner, but something told me that dinners had been missing for many days.

We were already quite far along the forest path when I realised Marius had said *your* dog.

I glanced down at the ginger and white pup, who looked innocently back up at me.

Something told me I'd got myself a pet.

"Storm on the way," Marius said some time later. The joyous Monsieur Duval had dropped to the back of the pack, which was fortunate, because he'd had no idea about which direction to lead us in. That hadn't stopped him from deciding to lead anyway, in the insufferable way that some people, who imagine they always know better than you, liked to do.

I glanced up at the sky, but there was only blue and white showing through the gaps in the russet canopy.

When I knew we were only moments away from cresting the hill and finding the body I'd stumbled upon earlier that day, I suddenly panicked that it wouldn't be there. I wasn't sure where I expected it to have gone - and even if it had miraculously got up and walked away, I'd be able to work out exactly what had happened - but it was a strange feeling to have... uncertainty. The note on the door and all it had claimed about me had cut deeper than I'd imagined possible.

The body was still there, looking exactly the same as when I'd left it.

I thought I finally understood why, against all of my reasoning, lunch had been the priority for these men of the law. The dead didn't need to eat, but the living had empty stomachs to fill. The only reasons to follow up on a suspicious death as soon as you heard about it were to preserve the scene from others who might come and destroy evidence leading to the resolution of a case, or to bring closure to worried searchers. In Sellenoise, the police knew that no one would find the body they'd been skeptical I'd be able to locate again myself, and no one was yet missing whomever this unfortunate man had been in life.

It was with these sobering thoughts swirling around in my head that I watched the police walk over and confirm my initial diagnosis - that this man was deader than a doornail.

Marius finished walking around the corpse and came back over to where I was standing with the dog waiting patiently by my side. To my surprise, thunder rumbled up above, a storm approaching just as the policeman had predicted earlier.

"Well…" he said, looking at me with an unreadable expression on his face, "…it looks like I owe you lunch."

4

FUNGI FEUD

Minding my own business was harder than I'd thought.

The day after I'd dragged two police agents through the forest on the worst scavenger hunt of all time was the day of Sellenoise's weekly market. With supermarkets and other shops a significant drive away, I was hoping to pick up some supplies for the dog I hadn't decided what to do with. The one I definitely shouldn't have living inside of my rented accommodation.

I hadn't asked about pets when I'd rented the cottage, but something told me that Pierre the pervert was probably not a fan of dogs found wandering in the wilderness. That was why the dog and I were doing our best to keep a low profile for as long as possible. So far, he'd eaten everything and anything resembling meat in my small fridge, and when I'd run out of meat, he'd eaten all of the vegetables, too. Basically, we were both out of food, and unless I went on an early market run, we'd be skipping breakfast.

"Do you solemnly swear to not eat the soft furnishings,

woodwork, or floor of this house whilst I am out bringing home the bacon?" I asked the dog.

He lifted his head from where it had been resting on his paws and gave me a look that said: 'Who, me? I'd never dream of it! And make sure you bring back some bacon!'

I sighed, suspecting that my words hadn't been taken all that seriously. "And if anyone creepy stares through the window, pretend to be a lampshade," I said by way of farewell. The dog blinked his golden brown eyes once, before lowering his head and shutting them again. A long snore followed what felt like a ludicrously short amount of time later. If there was an Olympic event for being the first to fall asleep and snore with comedic volume, this dog would get a gold medal.

"But... let's start by getting you a collar and lead," I said.

* * *

The market was packed with what felt like every single resident of Sellenoise. I'd checked the Wikipedia page that listed the population number, and that number couldn't be far off the humming hive of people in the square that was filled with striped awnings and the smell of roasting chicken. Sellenoise may not be a big town, but its weekly market provided an important shopping opportunity for so many of its residents. Stallholders knew that anything and everything could be sold in a town whose only commerce was the local butcher, the boulangerie and patisserie, a hairdresser, some bars, and a post office - which meant anything and everything was exactly what was on sale. All of this was good news for me and the dog, who was hopefully waiting patiently for me to return.

With a bright red leather collar and lead tucked into a bag, along with a small sack of food, I was ready to turn my attention to enjoying the many other stalls and discovering more specialities of this region of France, but I was distracted by my overactive brain, which seemed desperate to analyse any situation it could latch onto.

The murder had not yet been announced publicly.

Of that much, my brain was certain. The snatches of conversation I heard as I walked by a stall selling apple juice and cider still held whispers of 'the new woman in town', and as interesting as I thought I was, there was no chance that a person moving into town would take precedence over a sudden death. In a town this small, I wasn't sure if there'd even been a murder before now. Death from radiation poisoning, caused by forgetting to vent your cellar every year, was probably more common than someone turning up with an axe in their back. But what I couldn't work out was why the police were keeping a lid on it.

I looked around, feeling like a pink island in a sea of more autumn-appropriate browns, greens, and muted oranges. I clocked a dark blue jacket and saw Marius standing by the fountain, watching over the market like a faithful hound. He caught my eye and gave his head a single shake that was almost too subtle to notice. I would have concluded that it was a secret sign to stay silent about the body in the forest for a reason yet to be revealed, but that sort of head shake wouldn't have needed the kind of secrecy reserved for couples having affairs.

For once, I discovered I was in the dark.

Until I saw the new man in town.

This one watched the market like a hawk searching for prey, and when he turned his head and our gazes collided, I was suddenly absolutely certain that I was the quarry.

He had jet black hair that was a shade darker than Marius' own. It was as if this new arrival had been rendered in higher definition. The tattoos that snaked up his arms, visible below the short sleeves of his white shirt, were certainly in HD. My eyes were drawn to them, wanting to examine every one and know its story. There was one in particular that caught my eye... two latin words: *vindex magicae*, written in curling script. There was something about those words that sparked a distant memory, but when a man was looking at you like you were lunch - and not in the good way - you kept your eyes on his face and tried to figure out what you'd done to deserve such alarming undivided attention.

His black eyes were emotionless. As we stayed, caught in the moment like two rocks in a fast moving river, he lifted a hand and beckoned me to come to him.

Power hungry! I decided, unimpressed that I'd never even spoken to this man, and yet, he seemed to believe that he could say jump and I'd ask how high. The sense of entitlement was probably due to the badge pinned to his shirt, which bore the insignia of something related to security and looked police-like. Somehow, I didn't think he was a new addition to the local force, which probably meant he was here because of the murder.

"Madame French, this is Monsieur Martin. He is with our national security agency," Marius said, intercepting me on my grudging way over to the beckoning man and handling the introductions.

"It's a pleasure," I said, stretching my hand out for the other man to shake and putting on my friendliest smile. It was astonishing how often someone who didn't want to like you could be thrown out of their bad manners by a sunny smile. They would usually find themselves returning the gesture, and there'd be one more smile in the world because of you.

This man seemed immune to simple psychological tricks. He even hesitated before he put his hand out and took mine, shaking it once before dropping his own back by his side. His fingers twitched, as if he wanted to wipe them against his trousers.

"Are you here investigating..." I looked sideways at Marius, "...the incident from yesterday?"

"No, he is here to review of our police work. It is standard procedure, isn't it, Monsieur Martin?" Marius looked up at the other man, who crossed his arms across his chest and smiled darkly. I couldn't help noticing the way his biceps stuck out when he did that, and in spite of his work appropriate shirt, I sensed that this man was very interested in keeping himself in shape. In my experience, people in law enforcement who subscribed to the muscle-head way of doing things were not always the most law-abiding citizens themselves. They were the ones who had got into policing, not through a love of justice and doing the right thing, but in order to seek control over others and get a free pass to throw their weight around. Often in a very literal sense.

"Just try to pretend that I'm not even here," the national security agent said in a French accent that did not sound local, examining his spotless cuticles for a moment. His eyes found mine again, and I saw amusement there. It was the self-congratulatory sort reserved for people who believe they have got away with something and feel entitled to laugh at the clueless people around them.

"They could have sent someone less noticeable," Marius muttered when his new companion was momentarily distracted by some shouting next to a stall selling an impressive array of mushrooms and mushroom soup. "Pen pushers are usually fat and old. And I was told I had to cover my tattoos as much as I could when I joined the police. Daring to have them at all nearly got me booted out before I even began."

I had to hide my smile when Monsieur Martin returned his

attention to us. He was certainly not doing a very good job of blending in. His tattoos alone marked him as someone who was always going to stand out, and the way he appeared like a well-muscled pit-bull just made him more noticeable. When you added that to the fact that he was well below retirement age in a town with an average age of seventy - and most were on the far side of it - I was certain that Monsieur Martin was going to be the talk of the town, and I would be yesterday's news.

Or at least, he would be the talk of the town... until the murder was revealed.

I was about to subtly ask Marius if he'd made any progress into the investigation, and when the town might be informed of what had occurred, when the commotion by the mushroom stall grew.

"Simon Dubois, I know you had it in for Jamie, but you have gone too far this time. You're going to rot in prison!" a male voice that cracked with age shouted with remarkable force. The constant motion of the market seemed to stop. Everyone moved away, forming a watchful circle around the stall holder and the shouting man.

"I haven't spoken to that idiot in a long time. He's still sniping my best picking places, like the dirty sneak he is. If you see him around, send him my way for a good kicking! I waited ages for the chanterelle girolles to mature, and when I went to collect them, the entire area had been picked clean. It wasn't the first time, either! Stealing mushroom spots isn't a criminal offence, and you can't threaten me with prison for doing something to even the odds," the stall holder bit back, his weathered face and watery blue eyes scrunching up with bad feeling.

"You think leaving him out in the forest like he was rubbish for someone else to clean up is evening the odds? You're a sicker man than I gave you credit for. The police are coming for you, Simon, but being locked up doesn't go far enough to make you pay for what you did..."

The mushroom seller frowned at the elderly man - who was waving a very knobbly walking stick around in the air. "I don't know what you're talking about, Adam. And why are you suddenly here defending your boy? You normally tell everyone how disappointed you are in the little good for nothing."

"You know exactly why I'm here, you old fruitcake!" The walking stick was now making jabs towards the man selling mushrooms, who dodged with surprising agility for a man of his age. "It's because you killed him. You're a murderer!"

"Well, this is just perfect," Marius said close to my ear, drenching his voice in sarcasm. "I suggested to our illustrious chief of police, Monsieur Duval, that whilst we're waiting for a larger investigation team to come to town and take over the case, he should focus on being subtle, but you have to inform next of kin. The man you found in the forest was Jamie Bernard. Adam Bernard is his only local relative," he confided, sharing a startling amount with me. I thought it was probably due to him being nervous about an escalating situation that was being witnessed by someone checking up on his police work. "I suppose I'll have to make an arrest now," he murmured, shaking himself and walking through the throng of people towards the arguing pair.

"What's this nutcase saying about a murder?" Simon Dubois asked, looking at Marius with polite puzzlement on his face. "All I ever did was coat some bait mushrooms with something bitter to ruin the flavour after Jamie took my chanterelles, but I haven't even checked to see if they were taken. It was a harmless bit of payback, nothing more sinister than that."

I watched for signs of anything else, but puzzlement and confusion were some of the easiest emotions to fake. All I could tell was that Simon was either genuinely confused by the accusations being levelled at him, or he was a cool cucumber and was confused because he'd thought he'd got away with murder.

"Simon Dubois, I am placing you under arrest on suspicion of the murder of Adam Bernard," a new voice said. The crowd parted to reveal Monsieur Duval trotting along with crumbs of pastry still stuck to his shirt-encased paunch. He puffed as he pulled out his handcuffs and slapped them on the unresisting mushroom seller's wrists.

"Sebastian… watch the stall for me," the arrested man called over his shoulder. A man in his late thirties with reddish brown hair popped his head out of the back of a navy blue van.

"Is everything all right, Dad?" the new arrival asked, frowning at the crowd and the handcuffs that were on his father's wrists. He pulled headphones out of his ears, revealing how he'd managed to miss all of the action.

"There's been some sort of misunderstanding," Simon explained, his voice still level and cool - although, I suspected it could just be that way because the gravity of what was happening hadn't sunk in yet. "It would appear that Jamie Bernard is dead, and the police think I did it."

Sebastian's face turned to curdled milk at his father's words. He opened his mouth to say something in return that I was willing to bet would be a lot less civil than the way his father was behaving, but Monsieur Duval was already leading his detainee away. I thought the old policeman actually looked disappointed that he hadn't put up more of a fight. When he glanced at the national security agent for a split second, I realised why he'd swooped in and put on such a dramatic show. He was playing to the camera.

Marius walked back through the crowd towards me. "You'd better come down to the station as soon as you can.

Now that the cat's out of the bag, there are questions that need to be answered. We have to know everything you saw when you first found Jamie Bernard. I know you've already given us your statement, but perhaps you've remembered something else in the meantime? It often happens when the initial surprise passes."

I silently gave Marius much higher marks for police work than his gung-ho superior. He was a man who had an understanding of how the human psyche worked, and he was absolutely right that some details became clearer later when the mind had processed a shocking event that had overridden all other senses.

That was the way it worked for most people.

I'd already given them a statement containing close to every detail I'd noticed. I'd carefully curated it to not miss anything, but to also not reveal the high level of detail I always observed. It was tough to toe the line between being truthful, in order to give the police the best chance of closing the case, whilst not saying so much that it would arouse misplaced suspicion... or simply make them think I was a weirdo.

Well... *more* of a weirdo than they already thought I was for moving to a French town in the back end of nowhere.

"That's no problem at all. Would after lunch be best?" I asked, unable to resist making a jab at the laid back approach to work in these parts.

"It would," Marius replied, the snipe sailing straight over his head. "I should go and help Monsieur Duval. We were supposed to be waiting patiently for..." He trailed off and shook his head, glancing anxiously at the ever-watching national security agent. "Even murder doesn't count for much when you're from a tiny town. We'll just have to do what we can until the others come to help."

"It was nice to meet you, Monsieur Martin," I said to the

silent, brooding male - who hadn't said a word after events had unfolded before us. "Is there a first name to go with the last?" I did my best to twinkle, forcing down feelings of ickiness over this horrifying attempt to flirt.

His black eyes seemed to bore into my soul, but they revealed nothing. Not even disdain. "Lucien," he finally said, surprising me by giving an answer. He gave me one final dismissive up and down look, before he strode away through the crowd after Marius. I wasn't surprised when he didn't look back, but I'd already got what I wanted - a name.

Or more accurately, I wanted him to *think* that was what I'd wanted from him. In truth, I walked away from the morning market with more than just dog accessories and dinner. I left with the chilling knowledge that the letter left on my door had been no idle threat.

Lucien Martin was here to settle the score.

5

VINDEX MAGICAE

How did I know that the supposed 'national security agent' was here to follow up on the threatening letter I'd received? There'd been some obvious signs, like the way he stuck out like a sore thumb in Sellenoise. He'd also been waiting for me to turn up in the town square and had observed my actions with the vigilance of someone working a very specific job. I'd initially assumed it was because he'd been informed that I was the one who'd found Jamie Bernard's body and he'd wanted to question me, but Marius had confirmed that Lucien Martin was not in town for the murder.

What Lucien *hadn't* been doing was watching the police he was allegedly here to review. That was either incredibly careless of him, or due to over-confidence from his past successes. In case it was the latter, and Lucien Martin didn't care that I knew he was here for me, I needed to tread very carefully.

Luckily for me, I already knew far more about him from our first meeting than he would probably guess.

I pushed my pink-rimmed reading glasses up my nose and clicked the link I'd found on Google, using the rose-print vinyl covered laptop that basically contained my whole life. I frowned as I typed in the words from the tattoo I'd noticed earlier. "Fluff on a stick!" I muttered when the search results came back and I suddenly remembered exactly where I'd seen that tattoo before. Or rather - where I'd heard those words.

The latin roughly translated into 'champion of magic'. I'd done enough background reading when I'd been trying to fit in to the community I was masquerading as being part of that the latin phrase had sparked recognition. It was something whispered about late at night on the online forums. The Champion of Magic was a myth... a bogeyman... a finder of frauds... and judging by what I was looking at right now, someone had clearly taken the idea to heart.

Lucien Martin was more than a fake police inspector who'd been sent to make trouble for me. He was a social media influencer who used his 'mystical magician's powers' to help his clients get revenge on charlatan 'magic users' who'd wronged them. He was a glorified stage magician who combined sleight of hand with pre-planned moments to catch his victims out and shame them online.

"What utter nonsense. I can't believe my disgruntled ex-client would employ someone who's clearly a fraud himself to go after me. Why is it always the biggest hypocrites who shout the loudest... or in this case, have highly successful internet video channels?" I mused to the dog, who briefly raised his head from the bowl of dog food I'd given him and gave me a look. I interpreted it as: '*You* may know he's a fake, but are you sure he knows it himself?' - which was an excellent point for a dog to make.

Having discovered how ready people were to believe you

when you told them uncannily accurate information whilst claiming to be a psychic, I knew how simple it was to convince others that some things can only be explained by the existence of magical forces. In truth, I didn't think many were genuinely hoodwinked, but they were willing to believe anything that got the job done and came accompanied with a convenient explanation that no one needed to examine too carefully. Seeing as this revenge magician's current assignment was probably my own sudden and mysterious demise, quibbling over whether any 'real' magic ever took place was not going to get me out of trouble. Lucien Martin was a dangerous man, and when it came to dealing with him, I was on my own.

His social media profiles were only the public side of him. Who knew what kind of work he undertook in private... and how far he was willing to take things?

The knock on the door made me jump and slam my laptop shut.

The hairs which had been prickling on the back of my neck suddenly stood up on end, and I was sure - just for an instant - that my reckoning was already here. A second later, I recognised that the feeling was brought on by my own nerves, generated by uncovering a secret identity. I calmed down to a more reasoned mindset. The logical part of my brain said I should see who was at the door before jumping to conclusions.

The concave glass of the old fashioned front door distorted the features of the person standing on the doorstep. Only their hat was clearly visible through a less bendy part of the glass - a wide-brimmed floppy dark green affair with a pheasant feather pinned to the band at a jaunty angle.

Unless the new social media star in town was a master of disguise and changing his height, I was probably not about to meet my maker.

"Hello, how may I help you?" I asked, opening the door with a smile and a strong determination to expect the best - which I always thought helped things to go that way. Why worry when there was nothing to worry about yet? People liked to tie themselves in knots over things like that.

"Are you Justine? I've heard so much about you already. My name is Marissa Fennet. I... we, that is... a little group of ladies that I'm part of, noticed you're renting Pierre's place and I wanted to check that you're settling in okay. We residents of Sellenoise don't see many new faces around here, but that doesn't mean we aren't ready to welcome newcomers with open arms when word gets around! How long are you staying for?" she asked, bustling straight past me into the cottage. "Oh! You have a dog. That's a little untraditional, but we accept all types around here. He's sweet," the woman said when the dog trotted over and licked her hand, before returning to his place on the sofa.

I took it as a good sign that the dog liked her enough to say hello, even though Marissa was undeniably strange.

"Would you like some tea? Or coffee?" I added, remembering which country I was in. My visitor took off her hat, shaking out her dark brown curls. Winged glasses sat on her pointed nose, and behind them, her eyes were quick and observant. She wore a polkadot pussy-bow blouse and a dark green skirt - the same shade as her hat - over some sensible thermal tights.

"Have you got anything that's not loose leaf tea? I suppose that's a funny question to ask," she said, laughing as she bent down to undo her dark brown leather boots, which were worn, but well-cared for. They were the sort of shoes everyone should own a pair of. I'd never managed to find them in cerise, and when most of your wardrobe was pink or floral, you either matched or clashed.

"I've got apple and cinnamon, Earl Grey, or regular

builder's tea," I said, and then wondered if translating that last one literally would be confusing. "I mean normal tea."

"Earl Grey sounds lovely. I take mine with lemon and a spoonful of sugar."

"Just give me a moment," I said with a bright smile, already warming to the woman who wasn't shy about asking for what she wanted, exactly the way she wanted it. As I popped the kettle on, my mind automatically tried to fit the pieces of this new puzzle together. Remarkably, all I could come up with was that Marissa was eccentric, but didn't appear to have any ill intent towards me. For once, I was going to have to wait and see what it was that she wanted from me.

Because people always want *something*.

"I suppose you want to know about what happened to Jamie Bernard?" I guessed, returning to the living room with a tea pot, milk jug, lemon slices, sugar dish, two cups, and a plate of biscuits on a tray. It was my best educated stab in the dark at the reason why Marissa had turned up on my doorstep and invited herself in. What had happened in the market had been seen by everyone, and I was under no illusion that the locals wouldn't have noticed my casual stroll into the forest accompanied by two policemen yesterday afternoon. Curtain twitching was practically a sport in a town like this, and it didn't take a detective to put two and two together.

"Not particularly. Something like that was always going to happen to Jamie one day. You know how it is when some people walk around with a terrible fate hanging over them, don't you? Of course you do!" She laughed again. "Well, that was Jamie. I would never say he brought his own end upon himself, but no one in this town is particularly sorry that he's gone for good. Even his father is probably breathing a sigh of relief that his finances are safe again. That little display in the market this morning had less to do with Jamie and more to do with bad blood between families." She shrugged and smiled. "Anyway, let's talk about you! I want to know everything. Where did you come from, and why did you move to Sellenoise?" Amusement glinted in her green eyes. "You must be running from something *awful*, if you chose this place to disappear."

"Who says I'm running from anything?" I answered with a guarded smile, stirring my tea.

Marissa shot me a look that said we both knew it was the truth, but that it didn't need to be said out loud if I didn't want it to be said.

I tried to contain my surprise. Knowing things without asking was usually my role to play in a conversation. "I'm a therapist. I grew up and worked in England, but my mother was French, which influenced my decision to come to France. This is actually an extended holiday, rather than a permanent thing," I added, thinking of the man with the tattoos and the note on the door. If I had been running away, I hadn't done a very good job of it.

I was still wondering how he'd found me.

"I see," Marissa said, stirring in the sugar and taking a biscuit. She glanced over at the dog, who watched the biscuit in her hand like a very hungry hawk. I pursed my lips, suspecting we would have to work on the difference between people food and dog food. "What's his name?"

It took me a second to realise she was asking about the dog. "He doesn't have one yet. He's not even... I mean, I found him yesterday. Maybe someone is looking for him?"

"No one is looking for him," Marissa said, stating it as a fact. "So... he found you. That's often the way with these things."

"I'm sure he was on the lookout for any soft-hearted sucker and settled on this one," I said with a self-deprecating smile. I knew the French laughed at the English and their strange compulsion to save any furry animal that even looked like it might need help. It was not uncommon to see expats accruing an unintentional menagerie.

"A name will come to you," my visitor said, lifting her palm up and tilting it from side to side when a beam of light from the window caught it. She glanced towards the pane of glass and a line creased her forehead, as if a thought had suddenly popped into her brain.

"What about you? Have you always lived here?" I asked, curious to find out more about my strange visitor that the wind had blown in.

"Hmmm?" she said, turning away from the window in surprise. "Oh! Me? There's nothing to say, really. I'm the local postmistress, so I know everyone's business, and everyone knows to mind their manners around me, or else that business will be spread all over town." She winked salaciously, but I didn't believe she'd ever really do a thing like that. "If you enjoy peace and quiet with an extra helping of *nothing ever happens*, this is the place for it. Or it was, anyway." She rubbed her chin for a moment. "A change in the wind might do us all some good. It blows away a few cobwebs and it gets rid of any rubbish that's been hanging around."

"Rubbish like Jamie Bernard?"

Marissa gave me a sharp look. "I couldn't possibly say. This may be a small town, but I don't spend time with anyone I decide I don't like. There's no point wasting effort trying to convince somebody else to become a person you'd want to spend time with when there are plenty of decent folk around already. The others can go hang."

"It's my job to convince people to become better versions of themselves," I said with a lightly amused smile.

Marissa blushed for a second, but I was glad to see it. I liked people who were certain of themselves, but it did often come with the downside of never considering other people's feelings or opinions.

"So, your kind of therapy is the problem solving sort? It's not meditation, mindfulness, or essential oils?" she enquired.

I smiled again, well-used to people having heard of the more woo-woo types of therapy. When I'd labelled myself a psychic, I'd been in the midst of all of that sort of thing, and far away from the psychotherapy I'd studied after I'd discovered I had a natural affinity for it. I already knew that Marissa would have preferred it if I had been into essential oils. Psychotherapy unnerved a lot of people. It made them feel like you were taking a look inside their brains - something which they didn't seem at all bothered by when you claimed to be able to do the exact same thing as a psychic.

But that's all in the past now, I reminded myself firmly.

"People tell me their problems, and then I talk to them about what they've shared." That was simplifying things a great deal, but sometimes that was what it took to get people to let their guards down. "You know what they say - a problem shared is a problem halved!"

"Are you going to be setting up a therapy business here?" Marissa looked curious. She also looked like she had something on her mind that she wasn't yet ready to say.

I knew the signs.

It happened all the time when people first came to therapy sessions. I'd find myself talking about the weather until the final five minutes of a session when the elephant in the room would finally reveal itself. It was fascinating how many people left it until the last moment before they shared something real. That was why I always booked half an hour extra for every first session without my clients knowing it.

"This is only supposed to be an extended holiday," I repeated, but even I could hear the doubt in my voice. What did I really have to go back to in England - beyond making a return to a business I'd built on a selling point that had become far less of a white lie as time had passed?

This time, and this town, could be different.

Or it might have been, had my past not already caught up with me.

"Well, if you do decide to start offering therapy, I know plenty of people in Sellenoise who could do with it. If you like weird behavioural quirks and family drama spanning generations, you'll have the pick of the bunch. Remember... I know everyone's business." Marissa smiled in a slightly unnerving way, but even though there was a whole lot of weird about this woman, I found myself liking her. I suspected that you needed to be a little bit strange to enjoy living in a place like Sellenoise.

I'd probably be absolutely fine.

"I'll be sure to let you know if I change my mind. You're welcome to come here any time for a cup of tea and a chat," I said, sensing that this was the part of the conversation where my guest would drop in the big thing that was troubling her.

Marissa bit her lip and looked back towards the window for a long moment. Her fingers pressed together, making a series of quick signs I didn't understand. "Thank you for the invitation. This was lovely, but I must get back to the post office. Lunch break will be over in a few minutes. I will be back to see you again as soon as I can. That is a promise." She placed her floral-painted tea cup back on the tray and stood up, striding over to where she'd left her shoes by the door. She tugged them on without bothering to do up the laces.

Marissa grabbed her hat from the hook by the door and jammed it back on over her wild curls. "Really lovely to meet you, Justine. You must come over to my place for a visit any time you like. Just ask anyone around here for directions. They all know where I am." She hesitated for a moment longer, hovering on the edge of saying something else.

"Bother," she said in an undertone I recognised as someone talking to herself. "Goodbye!" And with that, she opened the door and made a surprisingly swift exit.

I was left in the sitting room with the dog with no name, wondering what I'd missed.

6

THE CUSHION CONUNDRUM

aybe you're losing your touch, I thought and did a mental run down of all I'd learned about Marissa Fennet.

My round cheeks plumped up into my usual smile when I drew my conclusions. I knew I'd got Marissa's measure. There had been more than enough signs. What I couldn't get access to was whatever had been on her mind and her inexplicably quick departure. I'd assumed we were in for the long haul when she'd settled into the armchair, as if she were part of the furniture.

I was still puzzling over that minor mystery when there was another knock on the door.

This time, when I looked through the glass, I found that my earlier worries hadn't been unfounded after all. They'd just been premature.

The revenge magician was standing on my doorstep.

I lifted a hand to bite my nails and then placed it firmly back by my side. No matter what Lucien Martin's intentions towards me were, I doubted he was going to stroll in and hit me round the head with a baseball bat. After all - that wouldn't fit with the skills he claimed he had, would it? I also didn't think that this would be the moment that he'd spring whatever trap he was undoubtedly setting for me. It was obvious that Lucien loved drama - and the more public, the better.

Suddenly, everything came into focus. I was thinking more clearly than I had done since I'd arrived in Sellenoise. The man outside my door was just another mystery to unravel - a man who thought he could outsmart me and possibly even imagined he had an impossible gift, but a man who would also undoubtedly follow the rules of his own habits and beliefs.

Which meant he would be predictable.

I opened the door with the ghost of a smile on my lips.

"It is my duty to inform you that I am now part of the team investigating the suspected murder of Jamie Bernard. Due to current understaffing, I'm here to check your statement and ask if there is anything else you would like to add to it," Lucien explained, his face doing a pretty good impression of a blank canvas.

"You're speaking in English. I assume that's where you've been living until recently?" I flashed him a bright smile.

He frowned, realising he'd picked the wrong language. "My work takes me many places," he said. "I am a consultant for a security agency who sends agents to anyone who needs them. In this case, I am working for national security in France."

As excuses went, it wasn't bad. His eyes barely flickered when I put him on the spot. I was curious about how, exactly, he'd managed to convince everyone who mattered that he belonged to the organisation whose badge he was wearing, but now was not the time to ask that question. Not when a different game was about to play out.

"Please come in. I'll be happy to answer all of your questions."

I kept my smile bright, but my eyes darted between the kitchen and the poker hanging on a rack by the fireplace. I'd never been the sort of person who popped along to self-defence classes for fun, or punched her way through kickboxing to release pent up energy - mostly because I thought that kind of person was certifiably insane for finding exercise enjoyable. I was someone who liked to use diplomacy, rather than destruction, to solve problems. And the smile that the man on my doorstep gave me - sharklike and hungry - let me know that he knew it, too.

Predator and prey, I thought to myself when he walked past me without taking his shoes off.

"I didn't think you'd have a dog," was the first thing he said.

"Was it not in the file you have on me?" I asked, only half joking.

He gave me a funny look but didn't comment. "In your own words, tell me about the circumstances that led you to finding Mr Bernard's body, and what you saw when you found him." He opened a notebook and looked at me expectantly.

For a moment, I stood there whilst the reasonable request processed. "Would you like some tea?"

I couldn't help it. People didn't usually make me nervous, but having someone in my house that I believed had been sent to make good on a death threat was definitely not on my shortlist of ideal surprise guests. Plus, you could tell a lot about a person from the drink they chose.

"No," he said, not even bothering to add a 'thank you' on the end.

A beat passed and I quickly realised he was waiting for me to start talking. As drink choices went, a refusal without an acknowledgement of thanks was... well, it wasn't good.

I answered his first question on autopilot, most of my

brain's processing power taken up with wondering why this man hadn't accepted any offers of hospitality. I knew he was here to do a job - although probably not the one he was pretending to do - but that was no reason to refuse the offer of a drink so bluntly. If I'd been casing someone's house in preparation for doing something nasty to them, I would have still been polite enough to accept a cup of tea. I probably wouldn't have drunk it out of guilt, but I would never have been *rude.*

"What did you just say?" the fake national security agent asked.

I frowned, trying to listen back to the words that had fallen out of my own mouth without me listening to them. "I said... there were mushrooms scattered on the body?"

"Before that. You said that you *sensed* that the man was a member of the local council."

"Did I?" I said, playing for time. This was what I got for letting my brain run away with me whilst my mouth ran in a different direction. I'd been on fake psychic autopilot. "I didn't mean that literally, of course. I just saw a badge on his shirt. It didn't occur to me at the time, but I saw the same initials on the mairie - the town hall, that is - when I was at the market this morning. I suppose I must have put two and two together without even realising." I smiled as vacantly as I could, doing my best to seem like an airhead who'd got her words in a tangle.

Lucien Martin made a tiny note in his notebook, but I could tell he wasn't convinced. He also wasn't sure of exactly what I was hiding. I observed that much from the way he behaved so guardedly around me. He'd even been reluctant to let me shake his hand for longer than an instant when we'd first met this morning.

"You didn't *feel* anything else at the scene of the crime?"

he pressed, his dark eyes analysing me so closely I thought he could probably pick out every pore.

"You mean… like an ominous feeling?"

He nodded, slipping up by looking hungry.

"Yes… I had an ominous feeling that something was badly wrong when I found a dead body out in the middle of nowhere." Now it was my turn to look at him like he was an idiot. Honestly, did some psychics really go around telling people they had *ominous feelings*, and people ate that rubbish up? The only real ominous feelings were surely experienced by their clients' financial advisors.

"Can I use your bathroom?"

The abrupt change in conversational topic threw me completely. I nodded and indicated that it was upstairs. The single bathroom in the little cottage was a room right across from the open plan bedroom upstairs. The only big secret to be found up there was my collection of mini-crocheted figures from popular culture. I'd made the entire cast of *Star Wars*. Crocheting was a hobby I enjoyed because of the way your mind could run free whilst you hooked your way around in a circle. If anything, I actually found it easier to think clearly whilst I was making my tiny toys.

I blinked and realised I needed to do some thinking right now whilst my unwanted guest was otherwise engaged. I'd slipped up once so far, but not enough to get me into real trouble. In any case, if this man truly was here to expose me as a fraud, he'd already know about everything I'd claimed to be because his new employer would have briefed him.

He's just trying to work out if you're the real deal, my mind whispered to me. And I wondered which conclusion would serve me better.

"Someone will be in touch if there are any further ques-tions," Lucien said, breezing right past me and pulling open my front door without a single look backwards. The sound of the door slamming shut seemed to echo through the house. I glanced at the dog, and he looked back at me with an equally baffled expression.

"Huh," I muttered.

Lucien Martin had gone from looking at me like I was a fluffy mouse about to be consumed by a python, to treating me like I was a piece of chewing gum on the street - not worthy of a second more of his attention. All in all, I'd never seen such an obvious sign of a man who believed his purpose here was already a job well done.

Which meant there was probably something nasty waiting for me upstairs.

I dithered in the sitting room for a while longer. My first horrible thought was that he must have left a bomb up there, which would explain his sudden desire to get the heck out of my house. For a moment, I panicked, wondering if I should be running down the street screaming at people to evacuate because it was about to explode. Only the fear of being known forever as 'that crazy English lady who imagined a bomb in her house' stopped me - which was ridiculous really, because I'd just chosen potential death over potential embarrassment.

Cursing my British inability to do anything that might be considered out of sorts or alarmist, I did the totally logical thing and strapped sofa cushions to my body using the bungee luggage straps I'd brought with me when I'd travelled and had conveniently left on the mantelpiece. By the time I'd got into my unusual outfit, I was starting to wonder if I'd jumped to the wrong conclusion.

There'd been no panic or urgency in Lucien Martin's eyes when he'd left the cottage - signs someone alarmed by an incendiary device they'd left behind would have been likely to exhibit. Plus, unless it was a pocket-sized bomb, he hadn't been carrying a bag when he'd entered, and the outfit he'd worn fitted him very well and definitely hadn't left much space for concealing explosives. Not unless you got creative about where you put them. I giggled at the thought and slapped my hands over my mouth. Now was not the time for my sense of humour to play up, and something told me it was the nerves getting to me. I caught sight of myself in the gilded mirror above the mantelpiece.

I looked like an blobby piece of ham sandwiched between two beige sofa bread slices.

Do bomb defusers wear cushions, or is this an anti-dog bite outfit? I suddenly wondered.

I did some more dithering and came to the conclusion that, if there really was a bomb upstairs, it was almost certainly close to going off and I risked being caught in indecision forever.

"Still... it's best to be prepared for all eventualities," I said to the dog - who looked as though he was seriously reconsidering his choice of person to follow home.

I staggered off towards the stairs and started the climb. There was a heart stopping moment halfway up when a cushion snagged on the banister. My arms windmilled as I teetered on the edge of falling backwards down the stairs. In all fairness, the cushions would have come in handy for that eventuality, but the idea of being found lying at the bottom of the stairs, inexplicably covered in sofa cushions, by someone from the emergency services was enough to make me swivel with all the grace of a cat and cling onto the banister with both hands. Heart still thumping in my mouth from the near miss, I continued up the stairs, silently cursing Lucien Martin for ruining everything.

I stood with my hands on my hips, like a strange cushion covered superhero, while I looked around the open-plan upstairs.

It was spotless.

I was a neat and tidy person by nature. Everything had its place. My *Cath Kidston* duvet was pressed just as flat as when I'd made the bed this morning, and the throw cushions were still present and unmoved. I used a toe to pull open the door to the bathroom, but even though it creaked ominously, nothing jumped out at me. Nothing exploded either.

With a sigh, I took off my cushions, realising I might have overreacted when I'd walked up the stairs expecting to enter a room filled with more boobytraps than an *Indiana Jones* film. No poison arrows had shot out, and there wasn't even graveyard dust sprinkled in an occult symbol to let me know that I'd been cursed.

I snorted at my own overactive imagination. Lucien had only been upstairs for a couple of minutes. Had I really expected *The Temple of Doom* to magically materialise? A frown creased my forehead a moment later. You don't fake being a psychic without gaining a passing knowledge of the other weird and wonderful trades people like to peddle to the unsuspecting. That was the reason why my mind had tossed up the idea of graveyard dust, but there were other, less obvious ways that someone who believed in all of that hokum could make trouble, weren't there? Tricks that were designed to be missed to test the person the trick had been played upon.

I pouted in concentration and looked around the room again - this time, using my keen eye.

Everything had its place... which was why it was easy to see when something was out of place.

I found the first sign on the dressing table. A jar of baby pink, pearlescent nail varnish had been twisted, so that the label faced the mirror instead of the room. Most people would have assumed they'd put it back that way themselves, but I had an image in my head of the room exactly as I'd left it that morning, and the nail varnish had changed.

I walked over and examined the dressing table without touching anything. The bottle hadn't moved far. If someone had picked it up and tampered with it without remembering exactly where it had been, it probably would have been put back in a slightly different location, but I didn't think that had happened. Judging by the way the bottle was still pretty much in place, I thought it had been turned around by someone reaching an arm somewhere where it had struggled to fit, and just brushing against...

I mirrored the movement as I imagined it, finding myself with my arm behind the mirror that attached to the table. I peered around the back of the looking glass, but there was nothing there. I wasn't stretching far enough. I moved my arm down the back of the dressing table, where there was barely enough space for it. I heard the nail varnish wobble just as my hand brushed against a piece of fabric.

Bingo.

The nail varnish bottle fell over and rolled away when I tried to get back up. Unlike Lucien, my arms were more like well-filled sausages than muscular spaghetti.

I straightened up and looked at my hand to find out which prize I'd won.

The black fabric formed a tiny little sack, gathered and tied with red cord to contain whatever it was that lay inside. There was a white skull painted onto the fabric in a simple cartoon style. My knowledge of spooky television shows told me that this was some kind of spell bag. Somehow, I suspected it wasn't a lucky charm.

I shook my head at the ridiculous thing, trying to imagine tough-guy Lucien Martin tying the neat little bow on the bag. Even though the thought of the big man having an arty crafty side - albeit a twisted one - did make me want to smirk, I knew a first move when I saw one. My eyes scanned the room again. This time, it was a book that was a little too far forward on the shelf. Lo and behold, another bag was sitting snugly behind it. Something about the way this one was hidden let me think it had been the easy one... like he'd expected me to come looking for what he'd hidden in the room.

I held up the two little bags, wondering for a second what they contained. I was willing to bet it was nothing pleasant. The smell was musty, as if some sort of animal product was in there. I could have split them both open and gone sorting through the ingredients, working out exactly what these little pieces of bad news were supposed to do to me, but what would be the point of that when I already knew it was super-stitious nonsense?

The intention was clear enough. Lucien Martin was trying to psych me out, using a strategy he probably imag-ined I'd be predisposed to believe in... if I even managed to find them. Whether he believed in it himself remained to be seen, but I very much doubted that these two bags would be the last I saw of him.

"I wonder if he's serious about all of this," I mused out loud, gathering the sofa cushions and carrying everything downstairs again. The problem with believing in magic was not the disappointment when the things you wished for didn't come true. The real issue arose when the desired results were not achieved and the person who wanted some-thing took more drastic measures to achieve the same end result.

Judging by the skulls on the bags I was holding, the end result would probably not be good for my health.

"It's a bit chilly, isn't it?" I said to the dog on the sofa, who wagged his tail in agreement and trotted over to me. His nose immediately found the spell bags and he sniffed one before sneezing and growling at it. "Whatever is in here, it's not the dog equivalent of catnip, that's for sure," I said, glancing at the bags again. I bit my lip, tasting the cinnamon and sugar chapstick I'd bought especially for the autumn season. "It's cold enough for a fire," I decided, scraping away the old ash and stacking new logs in the wood burner. I picked up the box of matches and struck one, watching the flame flare bright and clean.

Whatever was in the spell bags made a great fire starter.

7

A CRUMMY CONFESSION

B eing scared is a decision.

It's true that there are moments of unavoidable panic in everyone's life. There's the instant when you miss a step on the way down the stairs, a cake slides off a plate, or you wake up with a jolt after falling in a dream. All of these things cause a little zap of panic that most people are not immune to, but being scared of something all the time is definitely within your control.

That's not to say that there is never a good reason to be scared. Of course there is. Knowing that someone was actively taking steps towards bumping me off was definitely up there when it came to good reasons to bite my nails, but I wasn't going to let that affect my life. Perhaps it was exceptionally stupid or naive to keep calm and carry on in this kind of situation, but in spite of accidentally stumbling upon a body in the forest, and discovering that an alarmingly tattooed man had somehow chased me across countries, I *liked* Sellenoise.

I'd never been a big city person, preferring quiet and cosy villages surrounded by rolling hills. When I'd started out as a therapist, I'd set up in Brighton just to get enough footfall through my door, but I'd never missed an opportunity to escape to the country. As escapes went, this one was pretty far off the beaten track. With a population of just over two-thousand people, Sellenoise was a great place to live a quiet life that found joy in the little moments. There would be no worrying about world news, or stock markets, or politics when you lived here - mostly because the TV reception was so awful that you were considered fancy if you had all four channels.

Not wanting to hear the news or keep up to date with politics might seem like a narrow-minded decision, perhaps even bordering on irresponsible, but I'd always wondered about the use of worrying about it at all. Some people had ambitions to change the world, and that was great. I just wanted a quiet life that actually made a difference to people. Not many people, but a few of them - enough to have done something that *mattered*. I also thought that if you wanted to change the world, you first changed yourself, and then you moved on to helping the others around you. If more people in power had taken steps in that order, I wondered if the old phrase 'power corrupts' would remain true?

I shook my head and took a big sip of my tea - this morn-ing's choice was blackberry and bay. The point was not that I'd come to Sellenoise to avoid hearing about the way the rest of the world kept on turning without me, and neither had I come here to flee an old life - even though I'd certainly made my fair share of mistakes; I'd come to France to start a new life and to see where it led me. This was my adventure… and I refused to be afraid.

After all, in my own story, I was the hero.

Which was why I was starting a new business today.

It would be done without much fanfare. After all, I'd only decided it might be a good idea to test the water after

Marissa had clearly wanted to get something off her chest but had backed away at the last moment. I knew that everyone had their problems, their worries, even in a town this small and remote. There was certainly a school of thought that might say I was doomed to failure, being an outsider, but I thought that might just be my biggest selling point. Marissa had confided that, being the postmistress, she knew most of the town's secrets, and I wouldn't be surprised if everyone knowing everyone made it so that any real secrets never came out for fear that they would spread through the town like wildfire. The residents of Sellenoise may not immediately warm to me, but I was the one person who would keep her mouth shut - because I didn't know their histories, and I didn't have any friends to gossip with.

That was my brilliant theory. Only time would tell if it proved to be true. I just needed to do a good job with my first few clients. Then, the rest of the town would surely follow them in through the door. That was always the rub when starting fresh… who was going to be the first customer?

I'd found a nice piece of wood in the garden of the rented cottage and had decorated it with paint from the little hardware store in town, writing out my qualifications and the service I was offering, so that all the curious eyes would see it when I attached the sign to some string and hung it on a handy nail above the door. I hadn't asked Pierre if he minded me running my business from the cottage, but it seemed like overkill to hire a business premises, only to sit there all day, twiddling my thumbs. In any case, I was certain he wouldn't complain if it meant more female traffic filing past his window. That man could ogle for England. Or in this case… for France. It just didn't sound as good in a sentence.

Even though the sign was a particularly brilliant business choice on my part, not much has ever been achieved by sitting around and waiting for something to happen. If clients weren't going to flock to me to talk about their woes and worries, I would have to go to them. That meant venturing into the centre of town to be a social butterfly and making an effort to meet some of the people I hoped would later seek me out in a more private setting.

I fluffed my ash blonde hair, making the waves a little more curly. A slick of fuchsia lipstick, and I was ready to take on the world - or one small town in central France, anyway. I smiled winningly, practising how I'd greet anyone who spoke to me. Part of becoming a community businesswoman was being a part of the community, and I needed to get my face out there. I needed to be seen.

"You're going to do great!" I told myself, feeling the little bubble of excitement I always got when I knew I was going to meet new people. Even if my books weren't immediately filled with clients desperate to dump their problems at my doorstep, this was my own form of therapy. Taking a holiday from the mess I'd left behind in England was important, but I needed people. Solitude was not something I intended to spend my life in, with the exception of a few long walks in the woods. With a bit of luck, I'd find some lovely new acquaintances today. With the exception of Marissa, it wouldn't take a lot to improve upon the few that I'd already met. *Especially when one of them is trying to get rid of you*, I mentally added, glancing at the fireplace. No trace remained of the bags I'd used as firelighters. If only the same thing could be said for the one responsible for putting them in my house in the first place.

The dog yipped when I pulled on my cerise ankle boots with the bright silver buckles. I looked at him in astonishment for a moment, before realising he probably wanted to be out and about. I'd given him free rein of the garden, but I was forgetting that he was a dog. He wanted to be with his person. And that person, for reasons beyond my understanding, was me.

I considered him and he looked back, his golden eyes promising that he would be good and definitely wasn't going to make a nuisance of himself in any way, shape, or form. As an expert in psychology, I really shouldn't have fallen for puppy dog eyes, but somehow, I found myself walking down the hill towards the town square with a bouncy dog in tow. Hopefully, my future clients didn't mind sharing their secrets with a side serving of friendly dog saliva, or I'd be out of luck.

"Bonjour!" I greeted the man behind the bar, who was wiping a glass with a rag that hadn't been washed this century. I noted that the coffee cups looked cleaner, and the only plausible reason that his clients hadn't yet died of dysentery was surely due to the violently strong alcohol that was used to fill the aforementioned glasses. "Would you mind if I pinned a leaflet up on your board? I'm new in town. I'm a therapist, hoping to reach prospective clients in the area. A problem shared is a problem halved!" I added brightly, smiling like a lunatic at a man whose face was about as cheerful as wallpaper paste. Sometimes the smile trick worked and it got people to mirror your mood, but there was something about my current company that made me think he probably only cracked a grin when someone handed over a hundred euro note and told him to keep the change.

"What drink?" he asked, barely looking up from the glass he was polishing. I thought it might actually be getting dirtier.

"Oh! Do I order a drink and then...?" I trailed off, wondering if I'd missed some unseen social cue. I was usually perfect at picking up on hidden messages, but for once, I felt myself flounder. "*Café au lait*, please," I said at last, still watching for any hint that I could trot over to the notice board by the bar and pin up the leaflet that I'd printed using my neat little portable printer without being shot in the back by the double barrel shotgun hanging on the wall behind the bar. The fact that it had been mounted next to the stuffed head of a cross-eyed deer wearing a straw boater hinted that it could just be someone's misguided idea of what passed for interior design around here, but I didn't want to take any chances.

"I'll just go and wait at a table outside," I said, feeling like I may as well have been talking to the deer for all the response I received.

I'd wondered why the front terrace was so busy, in spite of the chilling wind that whistled across the square, tossing leaves and empty conker shells with it. Now the answer was clear - everyone wanted to avoid the personality that lurked within the dark domain of the bar. *You win some, you lose some,* I thought as I sat down at an empty table. *Not everyone is going to be your friend,* a voice whispered in my head, reminding me of a hard truth I'd learned from a young age. Everyone had their own personal weaknesses. Mine was wanting to be liked.

"Woof!"

I looked down at the dog, who wagged his tail and seemed to say: 'I like you, best buddy... and also can you throw me down that half-eaten croissant someone left behind on the table? I'm starving!'.

"It's bad for your health," I told the dog, who promptly put on the puppy dog eyes again. With a sigh, I casually flicked the flaky pastry off the edge. It fell into the dark abyss of the dog's mouth - gone in a flash. My eyes scanned the terrace and I discovered that someone had witnessed my moment of weakness.

A man with brown hair cropped a couple of inches from his head, but curling and fuzzy, was smiling jovially at me.

His cheeks were rounded and his light blue linen shirt bulged a little at the waist where the beginnings of a paunch spilled over the casual navy chinos he was wearing. My gaze was drawn by the little badge pinned to his collar, before it travelled up and met a pair of the kindest eyes I'd ever seen. They were warm and brown, and I knew right away I'd found someone that I could talk to in Sellenoise. Even as I was making my initial observations, he'd stood up and wandered over, carrying another pastry and the leather-bound diary he'd had on his table.

"Someone's hungry," he said, smiling up at me whilst delivering the treat to my incredibly grateful dog. "What's his name?" he added, reminding me of the fact that I really needed to get on and think of one.

"I'm still thinking of a good name," I confessed to the man, who was smiling down at me like we were already best friends. "Any suggestions would be great."

"I'll have a think. I'm Gabriel, by the way. Gabriel Sevres." He extended a hand and I shook it, feeling the warmth wrap around me and travel up my arm.

"You're the mayor, aren't you?" I said, hazarding a guess.

Okay - so it wasn't a guess. The badge on his collar bore the crest of the town and the same initials as the one Jamie Bernard had been wearing when he'd died. The only difference was that the French word for 'mayor' was written on this one.

"How did you know that?" he asked, the smile widening. "I guess it's what being the mayor does to you - everyone knows who you are! In this little town, I'm the big cheese." He winked to show he wasn't being at all serious.

I found I was smiling and laughing with my new acquaintance. "I'm Justine French, the new resident therapist," I couldn't resist adding when I introduced myself.

"Therapist?" Gabriel said, rubbing his chin thoughtfully

and looking impressed. "We're probably long overdue one of those around here. You'll have centuries of family knots to untie, mark my words. Still… more problems, more money. Isn't that what they say?"

"I always hope I can help those who need it," I replied mildly, having spent enough time considering the conundrum of taking money for doing what was essentially a good deed. In the end, I'd found my ways to justify it, and it largely centred on the fact that people seldom valued anything that was given for free. Also, I had rent to pay and needed food to eat. It was too bad that my practice in England had never got to the 'paying its way' stage before the psychic thing had happened. Then, I'd been paying my rent many times over, but without it being entirely morally defensible.

This time… things will be different, I reminded myself, trying to forget about the way my problems had already followed me here in the shape of a phoney national security agent and his unusual idea of getting revenge.

"I'm sure you do," the mayor readily agreed, beaming at the barman when he came over to deliver the coffee I'd ordered. Even the mayor couldn't crack that egg.

"Be nice if some people actually worked, rather than lazing around in cafes all day," the barman muttered - very audibly indeed.

For one horrible moment, I thought the comment was directed at me, but a sidelong glance revealed a sheepish expression on the mayor's face.

"Thank you for your feedback. I'll be sure to buy a coffee machine for the staff of the mairie, so we never have to come here and bother you during breaks," he replied, managing to scrape back a smile.

This threat was met with another blank look, but I thought it was the unfriendly kind of blank, if such a thing existed.

"I don't think I'll be able to count on his vote in the next local election," Gabriel said when the barman had sloped off to wipe down other items with his dirty rag.

I glanced down at my coffee dubiously and wondered if anyone had ever got salmonella from a coffee cup.

"I don't sit in cafes all day, by the way," he added.

I looked up in surprise, realising that the accusation had got to the man sitting opposite me. "I'm sure you do the best job you can for the town. Obviously, as I'm new here, I can't offer a fully formed opinion."

He nodded very seriously, before breaking into a joyous laugh. "Spoken like a true therapist! Next, I suppose you'll tell me that my problems can only be solved by one person - me." He waved a hand and shook his head. "Sorry, I shouldn't joke about it, and it's true - even if it is a cliché." He rubbed his stubbly chin, and I suddenly got the impression that the mayor had something on his mind he'd like to get off it - just like Marissa had when she'd invaded my cottage and left just as suddenly.

As if reading my thoughts, Gabriel added: "In any case, this town could use someone like you. After all... someone has certainly got something to get off his, or her, chest."

It took me a moment to realise he was talking about the murder.

It was almost as though Gabriel couldn't bring himself to say the word out loud, so he'd resorted to body language and verbal hints that were designed to imply what he was talking about. "Still, the less said about that the better. I believe all of it is in the very capable hands of our municipal police force, and they've passed on the details to the gendarmes, who do an excellent job of dealing with the more serious incidents when they occur - which is very, very rarely." His brown eyes darted up to meet mine, suddenly worried.

I managed a thin smile. "You don't have to sell the town to

me. I've already decided I like it here," I said, surprising myself by saying it out loud.

"That's… wonderful," Gabriel said, doing a fairly decent job of concealing his shock. "How long are you thinking of staying for?"

A dark figure walking across the square drew my gaze away from the earnest eyes of the man who'd sat down in front of me. The dark script crawling up his arms was all I needed to see to know who I was looking at. It would appear that Lucien Martin didn't leave town until he was certain that his work was done.

"That will depend…" I said without thinking, my eyes still on my new arch nemesis.

Unfortunately, I wasn't the only one using my powers of observation.

"Ah, the new man in town! Just between us, I think our local chief of police is hoping that he'll decide the quiet life is for him after all and he'll take up a post in town. I, for one, would be thrilled to have him working for me. He's been such a help with our current difficulties."

"Has he?" I asked, suddenly remembering that the mayor oversaw the local police force in small towns like Sellenoise. They weren't supposed to investigate anything serious, just observe it and report to the gendarmes, who had special operatives that dealt with crimes like murder, but I was surprised to hear that the 'national security agent' had actually done a good job.

Maybe his best magical ability is the ability to charm people, I thought and smirked to myself - which the mayor saw.

"He seems to be a very popular man with a certain demographic," he said in that oh-so-wise tone of voice that lets you know that someone thinks they see something that you don't. But there was absolutely nothing to see here. Not a sausage.

"He doesn't seem like the sociable type to me," I replied dryly, thinking of the way he'd behaved when he'd turned up unannounced at my house.

"Maybe he just needs the right person to bring him out of his shell a bit," the mayor replied, pretending to go all thoughtful and deep, whilst his eyes sparkled at me like the helpful sidekick character in a romantic comedy.

Great. The town's mayor was a glorified matchmaker, and clearly a horrible judge of character.

"I think it will be much better if he remains in his shell and maybe even considers permanently boarding up the entrance," I replied.

Luckily for me, help arrived in time to stop the mayor from giving me any more knowing looks or saying the French equivalent of 'the lady doth protest too much, methinks'.

My salvation came in the form of a woman with smooth, luminous skin that drew the focus in a way skin doesn't often do, unless it's notable for the wrong reasons. Her lips were rouged without being garish, and there was something classic about the way her hair was swept elegantly sideways into a plaited bun and her eyebrows were so neatly filled in without looking false. If I were to guess, I'd have said that she was not from around here, having a Parisian vibe to her fashion and face that probably didn't sit too well with certain locals. That made it even more surprising when she bent down and kissed the man I was sitting next to on the cheek in a fond and loving way.

The mayor reached up and took her hand, looking adoringly into her eyes. "Justine, I'd like the pleasure of introducing my wife, Maia. Maia, this is Justine. She's new in town and isn't sure how long she's going to be here for, so I'm trying to scare her off," he said with a twinkle in his eye.

Maia smiled regally at me. Whilst she had none of her

75

husband's warmth and effervescence - which I was sure must be the reason why this unlikely couple had fallen for one another - she was incredibly handsome and knew how to emphasise her features with makeup and clothing. I sensed that she was the calm and collected force backing up the mayor's bounce and enthusiasm.

"It's a pleasure to meet you, and I am sure my dear husband is doing no such thing. No one loves Sellenoise more than Gabriel."

"It's just too bad that Sellenoise doesn't always love me back," he muttered, before shooting Maia a guilty look. I knew I was right about the barman's words preying on his mind, and perhaps he wasn't the only one who disapproved of the mayor. For a small town, Sellenoise appeared to have a rocky political landscape.

"You can't please everyone," his wife told him pragmatically. "Have you told Justine about the town fête that's coming up? It's an autumnal celebration of the hunting season. There's a competition where you can have a go at shooting a bow and arrow at a deer cardboard cutout, stuck onto some straw bales. The winner gets an actual whole deer to take home and put in their freezer. Isn't that lovely?" Something about the curl of Maia's smile told me she actually thought something close to the exact opposite. "Gabriel's been working so hard on it all. He's had meetings practically every evening last week with the fête's board of organisers. On Thursday evening, he even went out into the woods with them to check over the deer hides that they've set up ready to catch themselves a fresh buck."

Gabriel smiled and nodded. "We care a lot about tradition here. If you decide to stay, you'll be welcomed to all of these events, and I hope you'll join in. I know it can be daunting moving to a new place and feeling like everyone has been here forever, apart from you, but there are more newcomers here than you might think. Maia hasn't lived here her whole life, and she's part of everything now! Everyone is always begging to come to her dinner parties. It's like being the *Kardashians* of Sellenoise."

I winced at the comparison, but Maia just smiled serenely. "You do have a way with words, dear," she said mildly, glancing down at the diary Gabriel had placed on my table, which had fallen open to reveal the dates of the previous week. I noted that the trip to the forest to check on the deer hides had been written in on Thursday and there were many other notes besides that, from scrawled telephone numbers 01 33 45 67 88 B and 07 8742 77 13 S to out of town postcodes 463104 N and 17696 E. It was the diary of a busy man, no matter what the barman lurking in his domain might claim.

"Darling, you're going to be late for your next meeting if you don't hurry. I got you this diary for a reason, but I sometimes think I'm the only one who uses it!" Maia gently chided.

"I have it with me, don't I?" Gabriel grinned back. "See? I'm more organised already. Oh-ho! Looks like something is happening at the police station," he finished, spinning in his chair at the sound of a door being slammed. More paint was probably already decorating the concrete outside of the building when Sebastian Dubois, the son of the mushroom seller, stalked away, his fists balled up by his sides in unconcealed fury.

A moment later, two gendarmes appeared with a man in-between them in handcuffs. We had an excellent view of them as they walked outside to the cars they'd left parked outside of the municipal police station. I got the distinct impression that the mayor had given this cafe his patronage for his morning pastry and coffee for this very reason. Gabriel might be the lord and ruler of all I saw before me, but that didn't mean he was above indulging in a little drama.

"He must have confessed," he said when Simon Dubois ducked down into the back seat of the car.

He did look like a broken man.

I frowned while everyone sitting in the square watched the guilty man being led away. I was so focused on events unfolding that I nearly missed Marius Bisset sneaking out of the station door and walking around the edge of the square with his head down and his cap pulled low.

"Can I have a word?" he said to the mayor in hushed tones when he finally arrived by the bar.

"Certainly! We'll just… step over here," Gabriel said, standing up and causing his chair to squeak loudly enough that heads turned away from the arrested man towards him.

Marius slapped a hand to his forehead. "A quiet word," he added in a voice that hinted of stress and frustration.

The mayor nodded and trotted after Marius' long strides as they made their way to a quiet corner by the boulangerie and patisserie - which had closed after the morning rush had already caused them to sell out. I couldn't hear what they were saying, the wind carried the words away, but it ended with the mayor looking pensive, before he dashed off towards the mairie without any further explanation.

I looked dubiously at Maia, who was still sitting at the table with me.

She rolled her eyes and smiled, closing the diary Gabriel had left behind and pulling it towards her. "You won't believe how often that happens. He's easily distracted, but he cares about this town… no matter what people say about him." There was a bitterness in her words that I thought was probably directed at those seated around us, potentially listening in.

"It was lovely to meet you, Justine. I'm sure we'll be seeing each other again soon - perhaps at the fête. A little word to the wise... make sure you get to the jars of lemonade or fruit punch first at any of these events. If you wait more than five minutes, the little old ladies will have spiked it with eau de vie. It's a wonder there haven't been any other sudden deaths in this town, caused by the consumption of questionable alcohol that's probably close to 100 proof." She sighed. "I suppose after years of it, you develop a sort of immunity. In any case, everyone seems to live to a hundred around here, so perhaps we're missing out on something. Food for thought," she finished, flashing me a charming smile. "You must join me for coffee soon. I'll send you a card." And with all the grace of a lady from a *Jane Austen* novel she bid me *adieu* and sashayed off to grace other fortunate town residents with her presence.

"Why do I feel like I'm the poor cousin and she's Caroline Bingley?" I wondered out loud.

"Talking to yourself?"

I turned around in my chair and discovered that Marius hadn't returned to the police station after his briefing with the mayor.

"No... to the dog," I said, pulling a face that implied he was the crazy one for questioning whether or not I was crazy.

"Ah, that makes much more sense," he agreed, walking around the other side of the table and sitting down. He cast a careful look around, but the gendarmes were driving slowly around the square with their guilty cargo in the back, and all eyes were otherwise engaged.

"He's confessed, hasn't he?" I said, able to read the utter resignation that had been on Simon's face from across the square.

Marius nodded, but I noticed the frown etched onto his forehead remained. His gaze was fixed on the place where the cars had been waiting throughout what must have been an arduous interview. An interview in which, somehow, they'd extracted a confession of murder.

"I didn't think there was any evidence that could have proved beyond a doubt that Simon did it," I murmured, thinking aloud.

"Well, Simon confirmed that the place where it happened was indeed a secret mushroom gathering ground that has been in his family for generations. For Jamie to have been there would have been upsetting, especially as there was a long running feud between Jamie and Simon over alleged spying and stalking, which had resulted in scuffles in the past. That was why Simon initially confessed to doctoring the mushrooms in order to put his rival off, but clearly, he did a lot more than that. This place must have been particularly special. Maybe it was one lost secret too many," Marius theorised, but I knew he didn't believe his own words.

"Did he also confess to being a collector of ancient weaponry?"

I knew I'd hit the jackpot when a cloud crossed Marius' tanned face. "No. As a matter of fact, he seemed pretty unclear about how he'd actually murdered Jamie. He was even unsure of the location of the body. It was only because Monsieur Duval told him that Jamie had died with an axe in his back and that there were mushrooms nearby that he was able to give a vague account of what supposedly happened in the forest on what was pushed as being 'his mushroom patch'." He shook his head. "It was one of the least convincing things I've ever heard in my life. What were you saying about ancient weaponry?"

"It's about the axe… I'm no expert, but it looked like something that had been found at an archeological dig and then restored to its former glory." I frowned at the memory of the unusual metal. "Bronze Age, maybe?"

"I just thought it looked old," Marius said, his expression darkening with a fresh storm front.

I tried to bite my tongue and tread the safe path, but what came out was: "Have you investigated this case at all?"

"We're the municipal police! Our job is to observe and report to the gendarmes. They've caught the killer who has confessed to murder. As far as they're concerned, the case has been closed."

He definitely didn't believe that.

Marius looked at me for a long moment with his serious dark eyes. "I need to go and check something." And with that sorry excuse for a farewell, he spun on his heel and stomped back across the square, like a disgruntled child being sent to his room.

"So dramatic," I said to the dog with a slightly amused smile on my face, in spite of everything that had just happened. It faded to a frown when I saw Lucien Martin materialise close to the bar and glance over at the patrons. He stopped dead when he saw me sitting there with the dog. The look of shock on his face would have been comical, had I not known that he was hoping something terrible had happened to me, or imagined that I'd be cowering at home, scared witless.

It was enough to inspire a smile to return to my lips, but with more teeth than before. I lifted my hand in a greeting and wiggled my fingers at him, as if I were completely clueless about the little bags of stuff and nonsense and his plot to get rid of me on behalf of my old client.

Lucien Martin was going to have to do much better than that.

8

AN AXE TO GRIND

"**W**hat is your deal?" The English phrase sounded strange coming out of the mouth of the policeman standing on my doorstep later that day.

I raised my eyebrows at Marius Bisset. "I'm sorry... *what is my deal?*" I repeated back to him in French.

"Who are you working for? Are you some kind of detective?" he elaborated.

I didn't reply immediately but looked pointedly upwards, where the sign hung proudly above my door.

He followed my gaze. "Therapist? Is that a cover for your real work?"

"I really am a therapist," I told him. In the past, I would probably be briefing him on the whole psychic thing as an explanation for whatever it was that I'd said which had made him suspicious. I assumed it was the axe.

Marius looked like he was chewing on something way too big to swallow. "How did you know about the axe? There were other things, too. There's something that makes me think you know an awful lot about Jamie Bernard, and yet you claim that the first time you saw him was when you found his body in the forest with an axe in his back and a handful of mushrooms scattered over his remains. You said you didn't know who he was."

So that was it.

I was under suspicion.

"I'm not going to lie to you," I began and tried to pretend I didn't see the policeman's right hand reaching down towards the gun that was attached to his leg. I supposed I should be flattered that he considered me to be worthy of that much caution. "In England, I was involved with the police…" I began.

"Involved as in… working for, or working against?"

"Working with them," I said, shooting him a look that said I wasn't amused by his not so subtle way of asking if I was a criminal on the run. "I was occasionally a police psychic."

Marius' eyes widened for a second. He rubbed his chin thoughtfully. "You're psychic? I suppose that would explain how you seem to know so much about Jamie Bernard."

"I'm not psychic," I said, doing my best to be patient. "I just told the police that because there was an incident that was hard to explain, and I panicked. There's nothing super-natural about me, or anyone else in this world for that matter, but I am pretty good at noticing things." I sucked air in through my mouth, giving Marius a quick once over. "Things… like the fact that you had egg and avocado on toast for breakfast. You play a stringed instrument, probably guitar. And if you're going to use fake tan, you should really wear gloves when you do it."

The police agent shoved his hands behind his back where I couldn't see them anymore. "You've just confessed that you lied to the police in your own country. Why should I believe you now? Perhaps you're indulging in some murder tourism."

I silently acknowledged that package holiday companies probably weren't missing a trick with that one. "I think you know that I had nothing to do with his death."

Marius' suspicion crumbled away, just as I'd expected. He wasn't a dim bulb, and he knew that you generally didn't stab someone in the back if there wasn't a grudge to be settled. Psychopaths attacked from the front, but people driven to kill - and more often than not, seeking retribution for a wrong they felt had been done to them - usually attacked from behind and with a furious rain of blows. Not to mention the mushroom sprinkle and the probable location. It all sent a message.

Someone who enjoyed the act of the kill and was motivated by that alone would have done things differently. I knew that much, because I'd been unlucky enough to have witnessed it before.

"Would you like to come in for a cup of tea?" I asked, now that I knew no guns were going to be pointed in my direction.

For just a second, Marius looked startled, but he stepped over the threshold and I got to work in the kitchen, taking his silence for agreement. He hovered in the doorway, watching as I put the kettle on.

"The gendarmes aren't going to do anything else," he said, diving right into the meat of the reason why he'd really come here today. He'd come to find someone who thought the same thing as he did - that an innocent man had just confessed to murder.

"Why did he confess?" I mused out loud, tipping the boiled water into two cups on top of the teabags I'd already put inside.

"You're the psychic, you tell me," Marius said, watching curiously as I got the milk out of the fridge, removed the tea bags, and added a dash to each cup, before offering him sugar.

"Very funny. That's exactly why I'm putting all of that behind me. I thought calling myself a psychic could help me to help other people, but in the end... it didn't work out that way. It was a mistake."

I bit my lip and thought about what he'd just said a little more carefully. "I'm sure he had his reasons," I said, meeting Marius' eyes and knowing that both of us were thinking the same thing. Simon Dubois was probably covering for someone.

While I had a shrewd idea as to the *who*, I'd need more to go on if I was going to make a prediction about the *why*. And making predictions was no longer my job.

"Someone needs to investigate this more thoroughly. It's typical of the gendarmes to take Simon's word for it, lock him up, and throw away the key without a second thought. They don't like being embroiled in matters in the small towns around here. The less trouble we are, the better - and this definitely counts as trouble and something they don't want to get involved in." He shoved his hands into his pockets and scuffed the floor with a utility boot. "Even the chief wants this over and done with. Just between us, he's never been fond of either man - victim or killer - so this has played out nicely for him. He also gets to take the credit for being the one to have figured it all out, even though all he actually did was inter-vene in a fight in the square. The man's acting like he wants a medal. Plus, he explicitly told me to stop asking anyone else questions. As far as he's concerned, it's done and dusted."

"Why did you join the police?" I asked Marius, who was currently sipping his tea angrily - which was really quite an achievement.

"I needed a job, just like most people around here. There

aren't many going." He looked over at me and sighed. "Also, I thought it would be helping my town. I was born and raised here, but I never really felt like I fitted in because my parents moved to Sellenoise to start a farm. Even though I've lived here my whole life, because they didn't, I'm still considered an outsider by some." He frowned. "I suppose I hoped that as well as keeping people safe and righting wrongs, it might get me accepted. Now I just think everyone is laughing at me for being fool enough to serve under Monsieur Duval. No wonder I got the job. No one else was stupid enough to want it."

I nodded sympathetically, but reading between the lines was a speciality of mine. Marius had joined the police because - in spite of what he claimed about being treated like an outsider - he cared about his town and the people who lived in it. If anything, growing up with the chief of police's incompetence had probably pushed him towards choosing a career closer to home, instead of joining a branch of the police who had more influence over crime.

"What's your plan?" I asked him, suspecting that he wouldn't be content sitting around and watching the wrong man be put away for murder.

"I've been banned from doing anything more. The gendarmes barely even glanced at the evidence because of the confession. Monsieur Duval was very clear. The case is closed."

"And you're okay with that?"

A muscle twitched in his jaw. He took a long sip of his tea, but that was apparently all the answer I was going to get.

"You're really going to let this go, knowing that there is someone in this town who deserves to be locked up - and it's not the man they've arrested?"

"He might have done it," Marius countered. "He could have been deliberately vague with his confession to sow doubt in our minds! Although, confessing isn't a conventional tactic to avoid being caught."

"But it is something a person protecting someone close to them might be driven to do," I reminded him.

We both looked at each other for a long moment, equally frustrated.

"I should get back to the police station. Even though the case has been closed, I'll make certain that all of the evidence has been filed correctly. I'm sure the gendarmes will realise they need it when the case goes to trial." There was more than a hint of bitterness in his voice, but there was something else there, too... something that sounded a little like rebellion.

"Pay close attention to the details when you do it. I find a lot of truth can usually be found there, lost beneath the obvious things that want to shout their story," I said, sipping my tea enigmatically and feeling a little bit like a wise master.

Marius shot me a look that heavily implied he didn't view me as his *Yoda*, but more as a pink and fluffy sidekick. He placed his cup down and walked back to the front door, hesitating after opening it. "Come by the station later today. I might need a few more psychic insights." After a final raise of his eyebrows, he was gone, leaving me alone with the dog and the uncomfortable feeling that I was getting myself into trouble again.

* * *

The square was empty when I took a trip down to the municipal police station late in the afternoon. The bar was open, but there was no one sitting at the tables. Presumably the barman still lurked within, like a bad-tempered bear in a cave, but I had no desire to poke him with a stick. Instead, I enjoyed the way the wind whistled around and the whole town seemed deserted. It was peaceful... calm. I felt my worries roll off my shoulders, which was why I'd come to France in the first place. *Everything is going to work out for the best in the end*, I told myself firmly, repeating a mantra I always found helpful.

The door to the station was open, so I ventured inside, breathing in a smell of old institution that reminded me of school halls and corridors. There were picture frames hanging on the wall that featured men - and only men - dressed in uniform, faded by different degrees that reflected how long they'd been hanging there. It was the town's legacy of past policing, and sure enough, the least faded of all the photos featured the current mayor shaking the hand of the chief of police, whilst handing him a certificate for thirty years of service to the town. I wondered how long Marius had been working here, and if he aspired to be the next chief of police and all that came with it... like certificates and handshakes from the mayor.

I was still smiling at the thought when someone I hadn't wanted to bump into walked out of one of the side rooms of the corridor I'd been about to enter. Lucien Martin and I looked at one another for a long moment. He appeared to be searching my face for signs of damage.

"Is everything okay?" I asked as innocently as possible. "With the murder being solved, I thought you would probably be returning to..." I pretended to frown in thought. "Where was it you said you came from? Somewhere in England, wasn't it?"

Lucien's expression closed down. "I didn't say. I travel around a lot with work. I'm not even certain where I was last, and it won't have been for long, so I'm not sure what you're trying to say." But he was sure. He was very sure.

I checked my peripheral vision, but we were all alone in

the corridor. "I know exactly why you're here, and guess what? I know what happens next."

He tilted his head, curiosity winning over his annoyance. "What happens next?"

I leaned in, making sure I smiled my brightest smile. No one would ever describe me as threatening, but I knew there was nothing more unsettling than a happy face in a serious situation. "I wouldn't want to spoil the surprise for you. We psychics know when it's better to let things take their natural course." I tilted my head and looked deep into his eyes. "But I don't think it's an ending you'll see coming. Not even with your expansive knowledge of tricks and sleight of hand." With another enigmatic smile, I breezed past him.

Or I would have done, had he not reached out and grabbed my arm.

I felt something like a jolt of electricity run through me, and not in a good way. When I looked back at Lucien, I saw uncertainty written all over his face. A second later, it was gone, replaced by the cocky smile that he'd been wearing ever since he'd first graced Sellenoise with his unwanted presence.

"Was there something else you wanted, Monsieur Martin?" I couldn't resist adding.

His hand lifted from my arm and he shook his head, allowing me to proceed without saying another word. Apparently, I'd won this round.

I waited until I heard the front door of the police station shut behind him before I emptied my coat pocket of the unwanted gift he'd left there. "Upping the ante, I see," I commented, looking at the single, but very large, black sack with another white skull on it. Subtle, it was not.

"Marius?" I called, holding the little bag in front of me like it was a particularly stinky sock. I poked my head into the first room on the right and realised it was an office. Out of curiosity, I strolled in and around the desk to take a look and saw a framed photograph sitting by a closed notepad and other files and folders that had been left for the occupant to sort through. Unlike most people who had a picture of their families, or even their pets, on their desk, Monsieur Duval had a picture of himself, standing by a very scenic lake with his hands on his hips and his legs spread wide as he surveyed all that lay before him. I thought I'd seen a similar image in the annual calendar of Russia's leader - except there'd been bears in it.

I was still lost in thought when I heard Marius calling my name. For some inexplicable reason, a flash of panic at being caught holding this little sack of nonsense overtook my logical reasoning. Marius already thought I was strange for knowing more about a murder than I probably should know, and even though I'd given him an explanation that hadn't involved supernatural powers, I definitely didn't want to have to explain what I had pinched between my fingers right now.

Which was why I opened Monsieur Duval's desk drawer and shoved the bag inside.

I pasted on a smile just in time for Marius to walk into the room.

"Is everything okay?" he asked, hesitating when he saw me leaning on the desk.

"All fine here," I trilled. "Just… got a bit of a leg cramp and had to stretch it out," I invented, acting out a few stretches, like I was a gym teacher from the 1980s.

"Right," he said, looking as though there were a great number of things he wanted to say to that, but he'd decided most were better left unsaid. "I, uh… might have some ideas of something we can look into. You know… as part of the community project we're working on?"

I frowned, wondering if someone was eavesdropping on

us. "Community project?" I repeated, before I realised exactly what Marius was worried about. "I saw Lucien Martin leave a minute ago."

Marius' shoulders relaxed. "Thank goodness for that. The man hovers around, like a wasp where there's ice-cream. I feel like I'm always being watched."

"How long is he actually here for?" I asked. I'd hoped that with the murder case supposedly wrapped up, and with enough spell bags to hex a rhino (theoretically at least) delivered personally to yours truly, he would be packing his suitcases and setting off to bother someone else with his 'revenge magician' stage show.

Marius sighed - far more loudly than I thought my question warranted. "Don't tell me you're *another* member of his fan club? We've been inundated with people reporting crimes ever since he arrived - all women, and all asking for the new guy to investigate whatever ruse they've concocted to get some alone time with him. It's making me embarrassed to come from this town. You'd think there weren't enough options on the table already! He's not even that good looking, and his tattoos are stupid."

I raised both eyebrows at this sudden outburst. "Why do you think you feel that way?" I asked and got an icy look in return.

"Don't you therap-ise me! I'm not jealous. I just think that everyone is getting way too excited over a new, shiny object, when some of us are just as good, if not better. I mean, do the tattoos really make women think he's mysterious or exciting?" Marius shook his head and looked angrily at the wall for a second before he added: "Do you think I should get some more tattoos?"

I tried not to roll my eyes too obviously. Marius seemed like a prime candidate for the 'A Positive Personal Affirmation A Day' calendar I usually gave to my clients at Christmas. "I think he comes across as confident. Over confident, if truth be told. He's also cold, and there's something about him that I don't like. I don't think he has much empathy for anyone, which means that - while he might be efficient in his work and has risen through the ranks by having a cutthroat attitude - it doesn't mean he's actually *good* at his job. I think we both know that police work is supposed to be about helping people and doing the right thing. Someone like Lucien wouldn't know the right thing if it slapped him around the face, like a wet towel in a hurricane."

"But... women like that, don't they?" Marius was really in a grump over this.

"No, they don't," I told him honestly. "Some women might be attracted to it initially, because they're hoping to see a softer side. When that softer side fails to materialise, and the man in question continues to be a psychopath, the shine soon wears off." I tilted my head at him. "Nice guys don't always finish last, you know. I always think the best thing to do is to keep on being you, and the right person will turn up... usually when you least expect it. I'm not a believer in fate or destiny, but it's funny how often that happens." Marius was looking strangely at me again. "I just mean, in general. Speaking generally. Not about anyone specific. You certainly don't need *my* advice. Look at you! You're great!" Wow, I was turning into the worst motivational speaker of all time. Normally, I never had any problems communicating with people. I wasn't awkward at all, and yet, here I was... putting my foot into problems that didn't concern me.

Problems... like this unofficial murder investigation.

Marius cleared his throat. "I've made an appointment with Damien Rue. When you mentioned that the axe was probably from the Bronze Age, he sprung to mind. He's got a thing about old weapons. The man collects them for fun and shows them off at town events. I didn't ask him on the phone, but I wouldn't be surprised if he's missing an axe. The question is… has he noticed it's missing, and was he the one who wielded it?" He glanced at his watch. "We should get going. I want you to come with me, just in case your psychic skills pick up on anything missed by my less-mystical eyes."

"You know I'm not psychic," I replied, unamused that this was going to become some stupid long-running joke between us.

"I know… but it sounds much better than saying you've got a knack for being nosy, doesn't it?" He grinned brightly, walking out of the office and calling for me to follow him.

Annoyingly, he had a point.

9

SNACKS AND SECRETS

"**D**o you know of a motive this weapons collector might have had for wanting Jamie Bernard dead?" I asked Marius in a stage whisper when we were standing on the doorstep of a dark grey house. It was coated in render, but the edging stones had been left bare. Although I found grey to be an imposing colour - especially when the house in question was out in the middle of nowhere, surrounded by fields with only a handful of horses for company - it had been nicely done. There was a barn attached to the house and I'd seen a flash of red paint poking out from beneath a dust sheet when we'd passed the cracked window. Damien Rue seemed to have a penchant for more than just old weaponry. He liked old cars, too.

Marius sighed, bringing me back to the present where I was standing outside in the chilling autumn wind waiting for a russet red door to be opened by a potential candidate for the role of axe murderer. "The thing about Jamie Bernard is that he was the sort of man who was always present, and yet, I don't think you'll find a single person in this town who doesn't have a bad word to say about him. You saw what happened when his father confronted Simon Dubois. He wasn't lying when he accused Adam Bernard of not caring about his son when he was still alive."

"What could Jamie have possibly done to warrant that much bad feeling?" I asked, astonished that one person could manage to rub *everyone* the wrong way. You could never be liked by all people, and it was really stupid to try - I knew that from personal experience - but for a situation to occur where everyone *hated* you usually meant there was a dark history.

"Let's just say our little town has its fair share of secrets, and they're probably better kept that way - a secret. Some things shouldn't be said out loud, even if they're true, but Jamie Bernard disagreed with that unspoken rule. I think he saw it as his personal mission to spill the beans on the residents of Sellenoise. Sometimes, I think he did it for fun, but I've heard whispers of other things happening and money changing hands. Plus, there was the mushroom issue. Our confessed killer isn't the only one with an axe to grind with Jamie Bernard. I use to receive reports of him spying on locals going to visit their favourite mushroom patches every time a new mushroom came into season." He ran a hand through his dark hair before patting it back into perfect position, using the glass in the front door as a mirror. "Legally speaking, there's nothing I can do. The mushrooms grow wild in the forest. Even though some people put down fertiliser - and who knows what else - to encourage their secret patch to produce more, they don't own the land. It's public. That means that, technically, Jamie Bernard was allowed to do whatever he liked... it just went against an unwritten code: 'Thou shalt not snipe others' mushroom spots'. Especially as he had a nasty habit of stripping these spots bare. But that's all just rumours."

"Why would he need so many mushrooms?" I wondered out loud.

"That… I don't know the answer to," Marius confessed. "It's probably something we should find out. It's another mystery to solve. That is… unless your psychic senses are tingling, and you already know why he needed a mountain of mushrooms?"

"Stop talking right now," I said out of the corner of my mouth at the same moment the red door swung open. A man with grey hair and mild eyes that seemed to smile out from behind his glasses was the one who'd answered. He put his hands on his hips to better show off the very nice red and blue striped dressing gown he wore - in spite of it being very early in the evening. I noted the little label sticking up out of the collar with some surprise.

"Guests! How lovely. Give me five minutes and I'll put on a spread. I think I've got some olives and a tin of really good foie gras somewhere in a cupboard. I bought it from the farm personally. I don't agree with all that goes into it, traditionally speaking, but… nothing can beat the taste! I'll crack open a bottle of wine, too. Come in! Come in! Let me show you around," he said, beaming at us, before turning and walking back inside, leaving the door ajar.

I exchanged a look with Marius, but he just shrugged and shook his head, following our eager host into his domain. I hesitated for just a moment longer, privately observing that if Damien Rue had killed Jamie Bernard, he'd probably treated him to a five course meal first.

"What do you think of the place? I decided to decorate it to look like a viking hall. Not very in keeping with the area we're in, I know, but when I converted this building from a barn, it just seemed to be begging for a huge fireplace. Once I'd got the banqueting table in and thrown a couple of old

shields up on the wall, the rest sort of fell into place. Still…
it's perfect for entertaining!" He dashed off, presumably
towards the kitchen.

I looked around at the room, which felt vast and unexpected after walking through such a normal-sized entrance
door. Wooden stairs led up to a mezzanine floor with glass
barriers that hinted how modern this conversion was, in
spite of the decor.

The decor, if it could be called that, mostly consisted of
weapons of varying age, but they were always old or ancient.
I tried to imagine the same thing but with modern guns and
knives hung like paintings and concluded that everyone
would think you were crazy. Somehow, when the weapons
were old, it just seemed quirky and quaint - the expression of
a hobby. And yet… having such easy access to so many
weapons and loving them enough to restore them to full
working order, so that they shone in the dim light that came
through the skylights with the smell of brass polish still
hanging in the air… wouldn't it be tempting to take them for
a test drive once in a while?

"Damien, we're actually here to ask you some questions,"
Marius said when the weapons enthusiast trotted back in
with a heavily laden tray.

"But we can also eat," I added changing my mind about us
needing to get to the point so soon. The food looked great,
and I was impressed by what Damien had managed to rustle
up without any prior notice.

"I'm sure you have an excellent reason for paying me a
visit, but I do love to entertain, so be my guests and dig in!
I've been wanting to meet you in particular, Justine, ever
since I heard we had a new resident," Damien said, sitting
down and directing all of his warmth and attention towards
me. "I want to know everything. Why Sellenoise? I picked it

by chance, but it's become my home, and this place has been my hobby in my twilight years. I've still got another barn in one of the fields out back that I'm going to convert into a house and maybe rent out to holidaymakers. I don't particularly need the money, but… it's nice having people around. Watch your foie gras!" he added, making me jump and stare at what was on my plate in case it had sprung to life.

A black and white paw had joined the toasts and pâté and seemed to be fishing around for the good stuff.

"That's Orwell," Damien explained. "I think my friends thought I was lonely after my son grew up and left to start his own life, so they told me this heart wrenching tale about a barn cat that no one wanted. He was supposed to live in the old barn I'm thinking of converting and catch the resident mice and rats to his feral heart's content, but just between us, I think I was misled about his feral nature. Or perhaps he misled everyone when he was rescued. He'd rather be fishing foie gras out of a tin than fighting it out amongst the rodents." He sighed. "I don't think he's ever killed a mouse in his life. It's probably why no one wanted him."

"He's lovely," I said, reaching down and rubbing the little cat's head. He purred like a tractor, winding around my legs and looking up hopefully.

"Don't be deceived. He's on a diet because he resembles a barrel on legs more and more with each passing day." Damien was trying to sound serious, but I could tell he adored the cat who had come into his life. "Now… what did you want to ask me about? I'm not in trouble with the law, am I?" He raised his eyebrows at Marius, the smile never leaving his lips.

"No, this is just a social visit," Marius said, managing to make it sound like the grating kind of social visit where you were forced to spend time with a disapproving mother-in-law. The policeman was not a social butterfly. "Have you noticed if any of your weapon collection has disappeared recently?"

Damien looked back and forth between us, clearly wondering if this was a joke. When he saw that we were serious, he turned in his chair and looked around the room. "Let's see... it has been a couple of weeks since I properly dusted in here. The last time I did more than just polish a few bits was before that charity soiree I helped the mayor to throw." He rubbed his chin. "It all seems to be here. Is this a trick question? Unless..." He stood up and trotted across the room, disappearing into a small wooden door off to the side that I'd imagined was some sort of storage cupboard. "My goodness! You're right! There's something missing from the guest toilet. It's an axe - it was probably used for chopping kindling in the Bronze Age. I restored it to the best of my ability, replacing the handle with one that I thought might be similar to the one it had, once upon a time. I'm astonished. I don't know why anyone would steal it. It has no real monetary value. It wasn't a particularly interesting example, or in fantastic condition when it was found. That's why I decided to restore this axe in particular. It was for interest only. Messing with an artifact tends to nix its value. No... if someone wanted to make a packet selling off one of my pieces, it would be the ones hanging over the fireplace there." He pointed to two impressive singlehanded swords, which appeared to have jewels forged into their handles. "Now, there's a very interesting story behind those swords..."

"Do you have any idea who might have taken the axe?" Marius jumped in before Damien could drift from the topic at hand.

"I can't say that I do. There's really no reason why anyone would have taken... oh. Oh dear. Are you trying to tell me that...?" Damien looked between us and saw our grim faces.

"Was *that* how poor old Jamie died? By my axe? I feel just terrible about it, if that is the case."

"Did you already know that was how Monsieur Bernard died?" Marius asked, his face serious. I noticed his plate was empty and he hadn't touched the food Damien had put out for us. I shrugged and helped myself to more, knowing that our host would be hurt otherwise. Plus, it tasted really, really good. If Damien wasn't the killer, I was going to do my best to make him my friend.

"No, I had no idea. I heard a rumour he was stabbed in the back. Honestly… that didn't surprise me a lot. That is to say - it didn't surprise me any more than his murder surprised me. It's a dreadful business, and not the sort of thing you'd expect around here, but…" Damien's face was suddenly a mask of apology. "I suppose what I'm trying to say is that Jamie wasn't always the most pleasant person to be around. When he was here two weeks ago, he had a bee in his bonnet about something. I saw him trailing after several people on the night of that charity do. He even bothered the mayor a great deal! His wife had to walk him away and suffer a conversation herself, just so her husband could play his role as host. No one seemed particularly happy to see him, but that was always the way with Jamie. You couldn't not invite him because of his place on the council, but all the same, you tended to wish he didn't accept. I discovered him and Sebastian Dubois out on the veranda on the brink of coming to blows. It was only when I interrupted to offer them another vol-au-vent that everything calmed down. Although, maybe it didn't calm down as much as I'd thought." Damien looked shrewdly towards Marius. I knew he was thinking the same thing that both of us had already wondered.

Had Simon Dubois confessed to murder to protect the real killer - his son?

"I'm sure the members of our illustrious police force

know exactly what they're doing. After all, there's no smoke without fire, or so they say. I'm only sorry that a weapon of mine was used for a purpose that it was never intended for."

"Would you rather they'd taken a pistol, or a giant sword?" Marius commented with such a straight face I was left wondering if this was his very dark sense of humour finally showing its face, or if he was actually being serious.

"Goodness, no! I never want any of my weapons to be used like that. They are items of interest from history, and that is all! Well, aside from a few demonstrations… and the bows that are used in the annual straw deer shooting competition. Will you be coming to that? It's great fun. Everyone has a go," he said, beaming at me.

"I'll have to see if I can make it," I replied, currently unsure if it was wise for me to invest too much time in becoming part of Sellenoise, in case I had to let it go again. Lucien Martin hadn't gone away as easily as I'd hoped.

"I see. Well, it was lovely to meet you," Damien said, smiling warmly at me.

I offered to help him with the plates, but even super host Damien picked up on Marius' large eye roll, and the way he kept looking towards the door longingly was quite distracting. I suspected any subsequent visits would be better conducted without him.

"I, uh… that is, will I be getting my axe back? It's sentimental, you know. It was actually the first one I…" Damien trailed off when Marius stood up and walked to the front door.

"Thank you for your time. We'll be in touch," he said, walking outside.

I smiled widely at Damien, hoping he wouldn't think I was *too* friendly with the policeman. "If you're ever in town, feel free to drop by for tea. I'm doing my best to get to know everyone, and I love the company."

Damien's reaction was immediate. All of the hurt caused by Marius' brusque behaviour vanished. "I will certainly take you up on that! It's been a long time since I've had tea made for me by a fellow countrywoman," he said, switching to English in a heartbeat. "Surprised?" he added with a mischievous glint in his eye.

I considered my answer for a moment. "I suppose I should have guessed from your penchant for renovation projects and love of history. I bet the French think it's unusual."

"They certainly do, but they all warm up to it once I get talking. It really is fascinating stuff. Anyway, I heard you're a therapist. Just between us, I think you need to work a little more with Monsieur Bisset. He wouldn't be my first choice of dinner guest." A wry smile was on his lips. "But, perhaps you can polish those rough edges, and then who knows?" The smile turned knowing.

I decided to pretend that everything he'd said had sailed straight over my head. "Thank you again for the hospitality. Sorry about…" I considered how to finish that sentence.

Damien raised his eyebrows. "I'm flattered that anyone would consider me interesting enough to be capable of murder. It'll be a great story to tell my dinner guests. See you soon!"

I walked back down the narrow pathway that led to the house with observations flying through my brain. The label I'd seen sticking out of his dressing gown had dictated that it had come from *Marks and Spencers* - not a French brand. What had clinched it were the swords he had above the mantelpiece, which I recognised from some long forgotten history documentary I must have once watched. They were Agincourt swords - so named for the battle where the English had won an unlikely victory. It was Damien's little joke against the French that few would notice. Damien's accent was perfect. He'd clearly integrated wonderfully during his time spent here, but some things he'd clung onto - like dressing gowns and the English sense of humour.

Had I guessed that he was English before his big reveal?

I'd known from the moment he'd opened the door.

* * *

Marius had not been a happy bunny when I'd got back to the car. He'd complained that I'd made him wait deliberately, and when I'd enquired if he had a hot date to get to, he'd muttered more choice insults directed at the national security agent in town. I'd spent the car journey back to Sellenoise wondering who it was that Marius clearly liked so much, and why on earth they would be silly enough to choose Lucien instead.

Beneath the rough exterior, I suspected Marius had a heart of gold.

I'd turned around to say goodnight and thank him for the lift back home, but he'd driven off before I could get the words out. I'd been left standing in the cold beneath the glow of a streetlight, wondering what I'd done to upset him. Evidently, that heart of gold was buried much deeper than I'd imagined.

With my mind on the dinner my dog was surely waiting for, I walked back along the short stretch of road towards the rented house, but something made me stop.

It took me a moment to realise what it was, but I knew that *something* had changed since I'd left the cottage. I'd seen it, but what had I seen? I looked around with fresh eyes, wondering what my subconscious was trying to tell me... wondering if I was walking into a trap.

The car I'd driven all the way from England was parked down a narrow alley by the terraced houses. My gaze was drawn there, and I realised what I'd noticed without knowing it.

Someone had done something to my car.

I approached with caution, my thoughts firmly fixed on Lucien Martin and his ill intentions. Was this another threat, or something designed to do me more serious harm? I tiptoed closer, holding my breath in case anything jumped out at me from the shadows. *It's not shadows that you need to be afraid of... it's people,* my logical mind contributed.

Even for a man who decorated his ill wishes with cute little skulls, the flower and leaf arrangement that had been laid across the windscreen wipers seemed... out of character. I reached out and touched the petals of a late blooming delphinium, wondering what it meant and why someone had left it there. *Starting the town's fête early?* I thought, wondering if decorating cars was a local tradition I knew nothing about, but it still seemed odd. Plus, I'd passed a handful of parked cars on my way along the street and all of them had looked normal.

I turned away and walked closer to my house, only to discover that it hadn't escaped the floral treatment. There were herbs in the corners the windows, and when I approached the front door, I saw the corner of an envelope sticking out from the letterbox. I pulled it back out and opened it, wondering if it was a followup to the threatening letter that had been left pinned to my door what somehow already felt like an age ago.

I glanced around, but there was no sign of life on the silent street.

The paper rustled beneath my fingers when I opened it, and I noted the different quality. The threat letter had been on normal paper - efficient and businesslike. Functional, even. This was thick and spoke of luxury. It was the kind of paper used to send a letter to a friend... *or an invitation to a funeral,* my darker mind suggested.

I unfolded it and read the words that had been written in handwriting I didn't yet recognise.

Beware of tall, dark, handsome strangers.

THE CABIN IN THE WOODS

I wasn't sure why Marius took me along with him to see Sebastian Dubois. I could understand why he'd brought me to see Damien, hoping I would notice a hidden detail, or perhaps relying on expats sticking together, but I wasn't yet sure why he needed my help to confront our new prime suspect.

"Okay, now I get it," I said when we were standing in the middle of the forest having reached a clearing after an hour's hike. I wished Marius had warned me of the journey we'd had ahead of us. I would have packed snacks... and maybe worn some walking boots. My pink trainers were caked in mud.

"Get what?" Marius asked, a muscle twitching in his jaw as we both looked at the dark walls of the log cabin that stood between the trees.

"I know why you didn't want to come here on your own. This place is creepy!" A heavy mist had infiltrated the trees and this clearing looked like something straight out of a horror flick - the kind which only had one survivor, and the survivor was traumatised for the rest of his, or her, life (or at least until the sequel released and they had to go through the terrible ordeal all over again in the name of entertainment). I glanced at Marius, silently weighing up my chances of being the lone survivor. Law enforcement never did well in this kind of situation. Script writers liked to string them up first.

"Don't look at me like that. We're just going to ask him some questions. It's perfectly safe. As Sebastian believes the case has already been solved, courtesy of his father's confession, I don't foresee any problems," he said.

"You sound like you're trying to convince yourself of that, too," I muttered, shaking my head. "And I don't know about you, but if someone waltzed into my house uninvited and accused me of murder, I might have a problem with those people after all."

"We're just here to ask a couple of questions. Plus, I have an ace up my sleeve," Marius said, looking at me thoughtfully. "Can you guess what it is?"

"Being armed and dangerous?" I hazarded.

"I mean… can you *sense* what I know?"

I surprised myself by being the first one to knock on the door of the creepy cabin, but even a chat with a possible murderer seemed like a better conversation than the one I was currently engaged in with Marius. I still didn't know if he was pulling my leg over the whole psychic thing, or if he thought I was acting out some strange sort of double bluff. I wasn't sure I wanted to know.

The sooner this is over and done with, the sooner you can get back to figuring out your life and what you want to do with it, I promised myself, smiling brightly at the surly man who opened the door. "Hi, we're from the…" I hesitated, wondering how to finish that sentence. Marius was a policeman, but I was a therapist. Plus, we weren't supposed to be here at all. Something like this should have been discussed during the hour long hike to get here. "I'm from the agency, and Monsieur Bisset is just here to check that you're all right. When a family member has been detained for a serious crime, it's customary for there to be a mental health checkup for those who are left behind. Can I come in? I have a few questions for you to answer. Then we'll tick some boxes and make sure that you're as hunky dory as you can be, given the circumstances." I pulled a sympathetic face and dug Marius in the ribs in the hope that he might do the same.

Apparently 'grumpy' was his one-size-fits-all option.

"I don't need any help," the man replied, lifting a large pair of headphones back over his ears and moving to shut the door in my face.

Marius' boot stopped him. "We also need to ask you a few questions relating to your father's involvement in the ongoing murder investigation. That part is not optional."

The son of the mushroom seller hesitated, eyeing Marius without any affection. "Fine. Make it fast. I'm busy." He turned and walked inside the house. I assumed we were supposed to follow him.

A low growl emitted the moment we set foot in the dark cabin. The orange glow of the fire somewhere deeper inside was the only light source. All of the windows had been shuttered. Even out in the middle of nowhere, Sebastian didn't seem to want to engage with anyone in the outside world. His dog didn't either.

Marius and I hung back by the still-open door, waiting for the owner of the growl to make him, or herself, known. We didn't have to wait long.

A fluffy white pompom of a dog jumped into the light, its needle-like teeth bared into something that was definitely not a smile.

"I thought it was bigger," Marius muttered, reflecting my own thoughts exactly

"Who's a cutie, hmmm? Who's an itty bitty sweetheart?" I said, bending and smiling at the angry ball of fluff. The white dog turned his nose up at me and sauntered over to Marius, cocking his leg over the policeman's boots.

"You have got to be... SEBASTIAN! Call off your beast, or I'll report it as a dangerous dog!" he yelled, trading in grumpiness for fury.

"He does what he wants. We have a mutual agreement. I don't bother him, and he doesn't bother me. Everyone in town would laugh at you if you tried that, so you won't report him. We went to school together, Marius. I know that you're trying to prove to everyone how tough and grownup you are these days, but to me, you'll always be the kid in the younger year trying to save the losers from the bullies and getting knocked on his butt for it. Now you're working for a bully and trying to save everyone in town from his whims. I guess some things never change."

Marius bristled but didn't respond to what was probably a fairly accurate summary of his life. "Two weeks ago, you were witnessed having an argument that nearly ended in an exchange of blows with Jamie Bernard. On the same night as your argument, we believe the murder weapon eventually used to dispatch Jamie was stolen from Damien Rue. What were you fighting about?"

I tried not to show any emotion but I couldn't believe Marius had immediately ditched the ruse of: 'We're asking questions about your dad' and jumped straight into interrogation mode. So much for having an ace up his sleeve!

"Oh, I see," Sebastian said, sticking his feet up on a coffee table littered with half-drunk coffees and the remnants of many microwaved meals. "You think my dad confessed to murder because he thinks I'm the one who did for Jamie, right?" Something that looked alarmingly like victory flashed in his eyes.

"Why were you arguing with the deceased?" Marius repeated, looking far more annoyed that his plan had been seen through so early on than he had any right to, given what he'd just said.

Sebastian shrugged. "If you're investigating, I'm sure you've found that there aren't many people in town without some argument or another with Jamie Bernard. He was trying to follow me and my father to our family's mushroom patches. We may have threatened to pretend he was a deer and shoot him, if he continued to persist with his actions." He shrugged. "Harmless threats. It was nothing out of the ordinary, I can assure you. In any case, I'm sure we'd have only shot him in the leg." He narrowed his eyes. "And we definitely wouldn't have used one of daft Damien's ancient weapons of boredom. I heard whispers that Jamie was stabbed in the back. Did they use Queen Victoria's letter opening knife, or Louis V's prized rabbit poker?"

"Do you think your father confessed to murder in order to protect you?" I asked, curious about the answer to a question Sebastian had suggested all by himself.

He shrugged. "I don't know. I've never been that close to the old stick, so perhaps this is his misguided way of giving me a chance to be a better son." He sat back and rested his clasped hands on his slightly rounded stomach. "I don't know about *better,* but I'll certainly be taking the opportunity to start a new life. Far away from this dump."

I narrowed my eyes at Sebastian, watching for the truth behind his words. I could tell that somewhere in the past, his father had disappointed him. Perhaps there had been some misguided discipline involved, too… something which had festered and turned rotten, along with their relationship. I thought that Sebastian probably knew that his father was covering for him, just as I'd suspected when I'd been piecing the puzzle together, but I wasn't convinced that Sebastian was guilty - not unless there was a motive I was missing, because the mushroom thing had obviously been an ongoing saga.

Could it really be possible that Simon Dubois believed his son was a killer and had lied for him... only for Sebastian to be innocent after all?

"So, you and Jamie Bernard definitely weren't friends?" Marius asked.

Sebastian looked at him like he was losing the plot. "Absolutely not. We did not like each other at all, and I was fine with that. It doesn't mean that I killed him. We kept our distance from one another, because when we did get to talking, well..." He gestured. "Things like what happened at the charity night thing would inevitably occur."

Marius looked confused, rubbing his chin in what I decided was overkill in the acting department. "If that was the case, then why is there CCTV footage of you and Jamie Bernard inside the bank in town together two and a half weeks ago? When I watched the tape, I saw Jamie take out some money, put it in an envelope, and give it to you. That's a strange thing for someone that you've just told us you didn't like to do, isn't it?"

Sebastian's face suddenly bore a close resemblance to the pizza growing mould in a grease-stained box on the coffee table. "That was just a transaction. People do business with people they don't like all the time. It's no big deal."

"In that case, I'm sure you won't mind explaining what the *transaction* was for - and before you say it's private business, I doubt you ran that money through the books. Start talking, and I won't report you for tax fraud." Marius really did have an ace up his sleeve, and he'd figured out how to use it. I was impressed.

Sebastian sat in silence for a moment, staring at the crumbs and spilled ketchup on the table before reaching a decision. "Okay, fine. I made a deal with Jamie because I figured that he was going to get what he wanted in the end anyway by being a sneaky spy and following me and Dad into the forest - no matter how many tricks we tried to throw him off the scent. That... and I hate picking mushrooms! I don't even like them! Look!" He pointed to the grim pizza. Sure enough, there was a shrivelled pile of little grey objects that might have once been mushrooms.

"Why didn't you just buy a pizza without mushrooms on top?" I asked and earned a glare from Marius for diverting the conversation.

"Because I like ham pizza, but the only way to get it is with mushroom or pineapple. Mushrooms are the lesser of two very great evils."

Marius looked close to tearing his hair out.

Sebastian cleared his throat. "I just wanted out, okay? I was going to take the money and add it to what I've already got and leave this place to seek my fortune in the big city."

We both looked disbelievingly at him.

"And by seek my fortune, I mean... I have a job offer in a games store as a sales assistant starting next week, but I needed to get money together to pay rent because I won't get paid for another month, and my father basically only ever gave me peanuts. Apparently, living rent free and getting free food is payment enough, or something like that."

I frowned at the man on the sofa, who was doing a pretty good impression of a spoiled brat, in spite of his not all that young age. "Why didn't you tell your father that you wanted a different job?"

"I was supposed to be taking over the family business and

becoming the new 'friendly local mushroom seller'. My father has a reputation for finding the best mushrooms and making the tastiest soups, pies, and pastries with everything he picks. He wants me to step into those shoes when he gets too old for it, and he never once considered that I might want to do something else with my life." He folded his arms and looked across at the pages from comic books he had framed on the wall. "I just want to make my own choices in life for once. I thought that if I cut a deal with Jamie and told him about all of my family's top secret spots - the ones he'd always failed to find - I could take the money and do something good with it. Something good for me," he clarified, as if there'd been any doubt over it being an entirely selfish gesture.

Sebastian bit his lip and hesitated before he revealed the next part. "I actually planned to double-cross Jamie. I took the money and told him about the secret places, but I also sent a letter to the town newspaper at the same time that should be published in the next issue. It reveals the locations of all the mushroom spots. Once everyone knew, I figured my father wouldn't have much of a business left, and neither would Jamie." He shrugged. "Before you tell me what a terrible son I am for robbing my father of his much-needed income, what you probably don't know is that my father has been selling the cream of his crop to Parisian restaurants ever since he took on the business from his father. I know I'm living in a slum, but my father has bank accounts stuffed with money from selling mushrooms at astronomical prices to snobby restaurants - he's just too stingy to spend any of it."

Sebastian scratched his head, making his greasy, reddish-brown hair flop down over his forehead. "It's also probably because if anyone around here found out what he does with the mushrooms, they'd go crazy. It's like treachery, you know? No one likes Parisians and having anything to do with them is practically a crime. Come to think of it, I bet Jamie was doing the same thing with all of the mushrooms he was stealing, except he didn't know how to be subtle about it. Anyway, I've never cared about the money. I just want a new start away from people who've known me since I've been born. Everyone thinks I'm this lazy slob who can never change. Even if I did change, they wouldn't realise it. No one gets a second chance around here."

"That's a nicely told story, but I have one problem with it. You and Jamie cut your deal two and a half weeks ago, but it was two weeks ago that you were seen arguing, and this supposed letter hasn't yet been published by the local newspaper, by your own admission. Why would Jamie argue with you if you'd already sold him the locations and hadn't yet double-crossed him?"

Sebastian groaned and slapped a hand to his forehead, as if this was all incredibly tiresome and inconvenient. It was a strange way to react to people who were borderline accusing you of murder. "Jamie Bernard thought he could have his cake and eat it. I should have seen it coming. It's precisely why I planned the newspaper thing. I knew it would stop him from trying to do exactly what he did, but I was too slow off the mark. I'd already decided to mark the letter as 'not to be opened until the week we're in right now', just so it wouldn't look suspicious," he explained, as if this paltry time delay would have made his plot any less obvious.

"Jamie collared me at the party for the mayor's charity and threatened to tell my father that he knew all about the secret places - and who it was that told him about them - if I didn't return his money." He snorted. "I'm actually surprised that he didn't ask for his money back with added interest - that's the sort of guy Jamie Bernard was. Good riddance." He coughed. "Not that I had anything to do with it."

"Even though he was murdered in one of your secret mushroom places?" I queried.

"How do you know if it happened in one of my family's secret places?" Sebastian asked, looking just about as shady as a person could.

Marius looked stumped. I realised that in all of the rush to nail down our guilty suspect, it would appear that the police had never actually confirmed whether the mushroom picking spot was one attributed to the Dubois family. There had only been the accusation levelled at Simon by Jamie's own father, and the police leading Simon into confessing that it was indeed the case.

"Did you really not test Simon Dubois over the precise location of the murder?" I muttered, shutting my eyes in frustration.

"He confessed to doing it!" Marius replied, but I knew he wasn't convinced.

I opened my eyes and looked with a clearer mind at the all too smug face of the man we were supposedly here to extract useful information from. "Is the letter you wrote to the newspaper still at their office?"

Sebastian shrugged - not willing to break the habit of a lifetime and actually be helpful. "Unless they thought it was a weird joke and threw it in the bin. It's supposed to be an anonymous tip off. I was going to blame Jamie for that, too. I planned to tell my father that he must have spied on us and decided to ruin our business out of spite. Jamie Bernard was going to get everything he deserved... which is why I should be off your list of suspects, because I already had a revenge plan in place. Plus, my father already told you that he put stuff on the mushrooms he thought Jamie had found by spying on us that would make them taste really bad, so why would he then kill him? It's obvious that we were settling the score in other ways."

"Or perhaps Jamie discovered your deceit and confronted you in the forest," I said, suggesting an equally possible theory.

The smug look disappeared from Sebastian's face. "I had nothing to do with it. Do I really look like the type to be running around wielding weapons?" He gestured to the game on the television screen in front of us, and then around at the room that was filled with comic book memorabilia and war game miniatures. "Physical activity is not my forte. Now, if you don't mind... some of us have an online game tournament to be getting back to. It's time to see if the satellite internet I paid an arm and a leg for is really worth it." Sebastian stood up and shooed us back towards the door, while his little dog glared at us reproachfully.

"Are you really going to let your father rot in prison for something he didn't do?" Marius spun around in the doorway to deliver one last question.

Sebastian folded his arms over his chest again, briefly covering up a yellow mustard stain. "He didn't have to confess to anything. It was a pretty stupid thing to say. If he thinks he's being the hero by protecting me from something I didn't actually do... well..." He rubbed his chin. "Maybe it's for the best. He feels like a hero for saving me, and I get to lead the life I've always wanted to lead. I'm not asking for his money, or for a free ride. I just want to get out of here. This works out just fine."

"But you were willing to take Jamie Bernard's money in order to fund your new life, betraying your father in the process," I observed.

"And now you're willing to let him go to prison - even though you don't think he killed Jamie Bernard and you're claiming that you didn't either," Marius said, making no attempt to hide the disdain in his voice over Sebastian's morally wrong decision.

Sebastian shrugged. "We all make our own choices in life. I don't judge you on yours."

"Yes you do!" Marius bit back, visibly furious.

Sebastian considered. "Then... I expect you to be a better person than I am, which is what you've always thought anyway. Bye," he finished, smiling insincerely and shutting the door in our faces.

There was something ridiculous about being kicked out of a house when the house was in the middle of nowhere. Marius and I stood on the leaf littered terrace for several moments before he broke the silence.

"So... did he do it? He didn't act very innocent, but maybe he acted that way because he's innocent... but also an idiot."

"I think that pretty much sums it up," I said, impressed with Marius' judgement. "I'm afraid nothing stood out to me," I added, doing a quick mental rundown of all of the things I'd observed. There'd been nothing that pointed to a murder having been plotted. There was nothing that pointed to much pre-planning of anything at all, apart from the transparent plan with the anonymous letter in the newspaper. And was a man who didn't know how to tidy up after himself capable of covering up a crime as serious as murder?

On the flip-side, you could never overlook that possibility that someone was more self-aware than normal. People like that were some of the most dangerous to walk the earth, and double bluffs were second nature to them. That sort of person was a rarity, but you could never rule it out... just in case. "We have to verify once and for all whether the place where I found Jamie's body was really one of the Dubois family's secret spots. Who runs the newspaper?"

"It's traditionally run by the secretary of the mayor - under his watchful eye, of course. I'm sure you can imagine the questions about bias *that* raises every time there's a mayoral election..." Marius shook his head as we walked back along the leafy trails with the smell of rain in the air around us.

"Then the mairie should be our next stop," I said. "We have to find the truth."

But when we arrived back in the heart of Sellenoise, all we found was chaos.

STUCK IN THE MUD

"What's happened? Police! Coming through!" Marius said, trying to push past the tightly packed group of people, who were huddled in the centre of the town square. Everyone ignored him.

"Allow me," a cheery voice said and the mayor trotted by. "Everyone stand back! Give space! And will someone explain what is going on?!" Gabriel's voice boomed over the muttering throng of people, cutting through far more effectively than Marius' attempt. Some people were born for public speaking.

A moment passed and then people did back up, just as the mayor had requested. A woman I recognised as being an assistant at the patisserie turned around to face us. "It was a terrible freak accident. I still can't believe my own eyes! One second he was walking down the steps of the police station, and the next, he'd been run over by a barrel of wine, thrown into the air, and trampled by Claude's Christmas pigs.

It was only then that people finally dispersed enough for the incident that had just been described so vividly to become fully visible. A smashed barrel of wine lay on the cobbles. The red claret ran everywhere, as if a dreadful massacre had taken place. Next to the spillage and broken wood was a metal pen that had been placed on the once grassy area in the centre of the town square. The grass was now a mud pit. Inside it were a bunch of surprisingly hairy pigs that had gathered around a large lump of mud.

It took me a moment to realise that the lump of mud was actually a person.

"What… what happened?" the mud lump said, sitting up and flailing ineffectively at the inquisitive snouts.

"Sorry! It got away from us," a young man in a flat cap said, taking it off and wringing it dramatically.

I was wondering why no one had moved to help the person in the pig pen yet when Marius rushed over and extended a hand.

"Monsieur Duval! I'll get you out of there," he said, always ready to help his boss.

"Get your hands off me! I don't need your help, boy!" Monsieur Duval replied, answering my initial question of why no one had helped him, whilst proving that he couldn't be that badly hurt after all.

Marius withdrew the proffered hand and suddenly looked very tired indeed.

"What a pickle this is!" the mayor said, moving to stand next to me and looking more delighted that something gossip-worthy had happened than concerned for the fate of his chief of police.

"This is unacceptable!" Monsieur Duval announced, briefly managing to get to his feet, only for one of the feistier boars to knock his knees out from under him again. "Get your trotters off me! This is an outrage!" he yelled, rolling around in the mud as he tried to ward off the pigs, who thought this was a fun new game to be played.

"Shouldn't be allowed," someone else muttered next to

me. "He's ruining my pigs' attitudes, getting them all excited like that. It's irresponsible, that's what it is. The law thinks they can do what they want around here. It's a bloomin' dictatorship!"

I spared an astonished look to my right at the most farmer-like man I'd ever seen in my life, before walking over to the pig pen myself. "Can you remember what happened, Monsieur Duval?" I asked, figuring that someone needed to check that he wasn't suffering any kind of shock from the startling incident. As the town's resident therapist, I was the closest it came to being equipped to do that.

His eyes narrowed when he beheld me. "You're to blame. Everything was fine until you got here," he told me.

"Monsieur Duval..." Marius tried. The chief of police waved a hand at him, flicking mud across his face. Marius looked like he was ageing before my eyes.

"I went into my office, discovered there wasn't a soul to be found in the police station, and then I came outside to find out what on earth was going on and... and... someone attacked me!" Monsieur Duval announced, managing to find his feet again and grabbing onto the metal enclosure this time to ensure he stayed upright.

"It was an escaped wine barrel. It was an awful thing to have happened. I'm terribly sorry," a second man in a flat cap said, looking at the spilled wine in such a way that made me certain that the apology was directed towards the wine that had been wasted and wasn't intended for the policeman at all.

"I saw the whole thing," the patisserie assistant piped up. "It really was a freak accident. You must have some awful bad luck attached to you. You should go and see Marissa about that."

"Nonsense! No such thing! This was a malicious attempt on my life!" Monsieur Duval blustered on as he tried and failed to lift his leg high enough to get it over the edge of the metal bars. In the end, he settled for rolling over the top and landing bodily on Marius, who'd been trying to support his boss. I thought Marius probably deserved a medal from the mayor for his dedication to duty - even when his duty was caring for a borderline nutter.

"Freak accident?" someone said from behind me, sounding curious.

I turned around to see Lucien Martin. There was an expression of curiosity on his face and... confusion. As if he didn't understand how this freak event could have occurred. His eyes found mine and the answer jumped into my head.

The little bag of nonsense he'd put in my pocket... I'd dumped it in Monsieur Duval's desk drawer. The last thing the chief of police had done was to walk into his office and then go back outside, whereupon he'd been hit by a runaway wine barrel and had landed in a pig pen.

Coincidence, I decided, firmly. I was not about to jump on some non-evidence based bandwagon and start fearing fabric sacks with skulls on them. Not when there were far more real things to be worrying about... like Lucien Martin's intentions towards me. I may not be willing to believe that Monsieur Duval's accident today was the result of anything other than events coming together at exactly the wrong moment, but I was starting to believe that Lucien Martin wasn't content with throwing a few magic bags my way and splitting town. He was waiting around to make sure the job was done. And I would be a fool if I waited for him to finish it.

"We need to talk," I said, holding his gaze with my own. In his eyes I saw the knowledge that he'd been found out flicker there. I was certain that he'd wondered if I was suspicious of him before now, but our dance around each other was over. I often told my clients that the time they spent worrying about a problem was far worse than actually tackling the problem head on and getting it over and done with.

I wanted Lucien Martin to be over and done with.

"No thanks," he said, his eyes skating over me and finding a more interesting subject in the form of Monsieur Duval trying to arrest the pigs.

"Excuse me?" I said, letting the surprising response get the best of me for a moment.

"I am flattered by your interest in me, but I don't intend to be in town for long. I've said the same thing to all of the others who've asked," he added, just so I knew that his politeness wasn't especially for me. It was the tactic of a man who was used to making others feel small in such a way that it wasn't obvious that he knew he was doing it. I'd met people like him before, and I wasn't going to be drawn into apologising for being a bother, or feeling snubbed.

"I actually wanted to talk about our mutual acquaintance. I believe you know Hilda March," I said, saying the name of my final 'psychic detective' client out loud for the first time since everything had gone wrong and I'd made the decision to leave England.

"Who?" Lucien asked, but he'd hesitated for a second too long and we both knew it.

In the midst of oinking pigs, a farmer yelling about the corrupt system, and grown men crying over spilled wine, we looked at one another very carefully. Lucien Martin was only just realising that he was no longer the predator stalking an oblivious prey, and I had just risked revealing my teeth and claws.

"You know what? I think I do have ten minutes free after all," he decided.

"Good decision." I led the way across the square to a cafe that was not the one where the barman lurked, presumably still dirtying up glasses with his never-washed rag.

La Petite Grenouille was the polar opposite of the bar across the square. Where its competitor was dark and forbidding, The Little Frog was a cheerful, freshly painted light blue and white stripe, with little frogs frolicking between the lines. Its position at the far end of the square meant it missed out on being the prime place for people-watching and gossip-listening, but I couldn't pick out a single other factor that would mean this beautiful bar lost out to the alternative option. It was frankly remarkable that its competitor was still in business.

"Helloooo there!" a man dressed in purple pyjamas said, flinging open the door to the bar, as if it were the curtain of a stage and he was making his grand entrance. "Welcome to *La Petite Grenouille*. I am Julien Beaufort, and I bid you to take a seat anywhere you please. I would be delighted to bring you both a menu and then, whilst you are deliberating, I shall perform a song from the opera 'The Little Green Frog', for which, this bar was named."

"I haven't heard of that opera before, but I'm sure it's lovely," I said, knowing that being nice to people you'd just met was always the right answer.

"Thank you! I wrote it myself. I am the creator and the actor in this one man show, and you will be my audience and participants. Sit down... sit down! I will be right back." Our pyjama wearing host rushed off. I thought I just caught him say: New people! I haven't had a new audience in forever. Hopefully they don't throw food at me this time...

Lucien blinked at me a few times as if to say 'What just happened?' but he sat down at the table as directed, and when several seconds had passed without anything else happening, he began to talk.

"Are you the real deal?" he asked, his dark eyes serious and searching. "In all my time doing... the job I do... I've never met anyone like you. I can't seem to figure you out." He rested his head on his hands. "It's intriguing."

"Would you believe it if I said I was the real deal?" I knew I was slipping into the therapist habit of asking questions rather than answering anything personal, but even after thinking it over several times, I hadn't been able to conclude whether Lucien took himself seriously, or if it was all an act. Had he fallen into the same trap as the charlatans he sought to take down - believing his own fiction?

Lucien sat back with a wide smile on his face, wagging his finger at me. "You are good. You're really good! It's almost as if I'm the one…"

"…Being played?" I suggested, all too familiar with the final exposé The Champion of Magic - liked to inflict upon his targets. I hoped that knowing the way he liked to finish things would be enough to save me from suffering the same fate, but I also knew that there were cards still to be played… and I had to figure out what kind of hand Lucien was holding.

He smiled again, his eyes still lacking the warmth that would have been there if we were friends. We were still opponents sitting on either side of the board, and I knew better than to let my guard down. "How much do you know?" he asked, doing a fine job of tiptoeing around the matter himself. I was aware that he was well versed in psychology. It was how he got his victims.

"I know that my ex-client employed you in order to expose me as a fraud and do everything that goes along with that sort of revelation. Either she paid you a good amount of money to go after me, or she made her case compelling enough that you believed I deserve this kind of treatment." I tilted my head at him, reading his expression. I already knew from his very public channel that he undertook both 'public interest' and private work that I presumed didn't end up plastered all over the internet, but more likely ended in darker ways involving more money changing hands in exchange for silence. "For money," I concluded, before adding… "At first, anyway. You're not so sure anymore, are you?"

Lucien's left eyebrow flinched - a sign I read as him being impressed with my words so far.

He leaned forward, his expression as blank as he could make it. "There is something I should tell you…"

"ON A STARLESS NIGHT CLOAKED WITH FOG, WAS AN EMPTY POND AND A LONELY FROG…" the owner of the bar bellowed in an alarmingly loud baritone voice.

There was a scraping sound as Lucien nearly fell off his chair backwards and had to grab onto an umbrella stand to steady himself. I blinked in surprise at the number of sequins someone had managed to fit onto a one-piece frog catsuit (how I wished I didn't have to put all of those words together).

"RIBBET! RIBBET! HE SANG ALL ALONE, ON THE LILY PAD WHERE HE'D MADE HIS HOME. THERE MUST BE A WORLD BEYOND THIS POOL, I WILL VENTURE TO FIND THE MEANING OF IT ALL! What can I get you both to drink?" he added in a completely normal voice, smiling brightly at us and whipping out a notepad from what I sincerely hoped was a hidden pocket in the garment he was wearing.

"Actually…" Lucien began, but I cut him off.

"Could I please have a hot chocolate?" I asked, wondering if I'd accidentally stumbled into a parallel universe.

"Black coffee," my companion relented, glaring at me.

"Right-oh! I'll be back with that and the next part of the musical. Ta-rah!" The frog man skipped away like a lamb in the springtime.

A long moment of silence passed.

"So, that's why this place is never busy," Lucien observed. "I can't believe you ordered! This was supposed to be a quiet conversation."

"I sincerely doubt anyone is going to overhear anything that's said between us. No one seems to get within one hundred metres of this place. It's a shame really. Such a nice little bar!"

"Run by a madman," Lucien pointed out, so deadly serious it made me want to laugh.

"You were about to tell me something," I prompted him, aware that the time for confidences may be fleeting.

He nodded, his eyes suddenly serious and focused again. "I wanted to say that when I took this case, it was for money. You're right about that. Then, when I came to this town and discovered a murder had taken place, and that you were the one who found the body, I took time to do a little more research and discovered you've been tangled up with police affairs for quite some time. It's actually how you got your reputation for being a psychic. And yet... when I asked around here, no one knew anything about your alleged extrasensory abilities. My biggest question is this... why would an allegedly genuine, and admittedly not unsuccessful, psychic move abroad suddenly and forget about all of the psychic stuff... only to be embroiled in a murder investigation again? Not only that, an investigation that my police sources tell me you know quite a lot about with no good explanation as to why."

He examined my face, searching for any sign of a reaction from me that might express guilt. "I have a couple of theories in my mind. One is that you're the real deal, and like many talented people, you've discovered that you can't keep everyone happy and decided to take a break - only, it turned out to be a tough habit to break and you just want to help people. My other theory is that you're an attention seeking psychopathic criminal who commits crimes that you then 'solve' using fake psychic powers, whilst profiting both financially and from the warm do-gooder feeling you get from being a hero. The question is... which shoe fits?"

"I bet I can guess your favourite theory," I muttered darkly, before adding: "Are those really my only two options?"

A hot chocolate complete with whipped cream and green white chocolate sauce drizzle was placed down on the table in front of me. "Thanks, it looks great!" I said to the bar owner Julien, who was now wearing a papier-mâché frog outfit that made him resemble a lime green bauble. I had a feeling that the bar owner would be an easy man to buy a present for at Christmas.

"Which is it? Are you a psychic, or a psycho?" Lucien asked, ignoring the man who'd brought him his drink. "Right now, I'm leaning towards..."

"OUT OF THE WATER HE LEAPT WITH A SPLASH, THE NIGHT WAS RIPE FOR A MIDNIGHT DASH! BUT NOT ONLY THE FROG WAS LIFTING HIS ROOTS, FOR HIGH UP ABOVE AN OWL DID HOOT..."

Lucien covered his eyes with his hands for a second, before looking seriously at the singer. "How long is this opera?"

"An excellent question, my good man! And the answer is... well... I don't actually know. No one has ever let me finish it," the frog fan replied.

"That's such a shame! I would love to hear the whole thing," I said with the utmost sincerity. While now may not be the opportune moment for doing so, I genuinely believed that everyone should have a chance to do what they were passionate about. That, and I was a chronic people pleaser who found it impossible to say no to others when saying no would make them unhappy.

Lucien made a sound that sounded a lot like the 'Noooo' a bad guy makes when they've been pushed off the side of a mountain by the hero of the story, fading into nothingness at the end.

The bar owner looked at him and Lucien coughed, realising he'd reacted openly. "I mean, we appreciate the entertainment, but we do also have pressing things to discuss. Could you..." He looked from my still-smiling face to the man wearing the frog outfit and partially deflated. "Could you tell us when there's an interval?"

And that was how we spent the next twenty minutes listening to the story of how a plucky frog left his pond and evaded a predatory owl, only to realise he had become lost in the big wide world beyond his home with no way back. When all hope was gone, he heard someone shouting for help and discovered another frog in mortal peril with a cat about to deliver a fatal blow. With a heart full of courage, the frog had leapt on the cat. The frogs had fallen through a drainage cover and were cowering below the ground with water rushing past them... which was when they finally looked at one another and felt their loneliness fade away.

"Love at first sight!" I said, applauding when the bar owner finished the first act with a flourish. "I'm excited to find out what comes next, aren't you, Lucien?"

Lucien's face twisted, like he was having a particularly painful torture inflicted upon him. "I...I..."

"Wonderful!" I finished for him. "The part where the frog finds a bowtie just lying on the ground and puts it on was particularly surprising."

"It's so nice to have new fans," the bar owner told us, clapping his hands in glee and dashing back inside, presumably to prepare for the second act that would follow the interval.

"Can we please leave?" Lucien said, looking about as desperate as I'd ever seen a man look.

"We haven't finished our conversation. I believe you were about to decide if I'm a psychic or a psychopath, as those were the only two options you put on the table. I assume both result in a bad ending for me? I strongly suspect that you don't believe in psychics, so you'll probably keep trying to catch me out, or psych me out using whatever is in those bags you keep leaving places. Alternatively, you'll expose me as a truly terrible criminal. They're not very inviting options, are they?"

"Maybe I'll be willing to reconsider, if you genuinely are the real deal. You've done the best out of anyone I've met so far. I don't let things get under my skin, but for the first time, I'm beginning to wonder..." He looked over towards the pig pen that was now free from invading chiefs of police.

I finished off my hot chocolate and looked reflectively at the last few frothy dregs at the bottom of the cup. Inside my head, I debated the merits of how good the hot chocolate was here against the alarming entertainment. Having said that, I had actually enjoyed the part with the bowtie, and I did love a good romance...

Lucien snapped his fingers under my nose.

"Consider how your social interactions make the other person feel. You'll be amazed at the results!" I said automatically, biting my tongue when I remembered the person I was talking to. Lucien Martin thrived on breaking social convention by publicly ridiculing people he deemed were deserving of such treatment. He was a self-appointed judge and jury.

I took a deep breath, considering what move to make, what version of the truth to tell. All I knew was that it should be truthful. Anything else would only pull me back into the life I'd accidentally tangled myself up in back in England.

But the truth could also get me in trouble and end up

taking me back there anyway... only to upset a lot of people who'd put their faith in me. It was a morally tricky situation, and I had only myself to blame.

It did not mean I deserved what Lucien Martin was dishing out in the name of 'justice'. There had to be some middle ground, and as someone who knew a thing or two about the human psyche, I was willing to take a stab at finding it.

"Sometimes, sensitive people need a break from being in the thick of it all the time," I began, treading a precarious line between truth and lies. "I thought coming here would be like a holiday. I did leave the country suddenly because of what happened with our mutual acquaintance, but I think you already know I provided the service I promised, and I really was sorry about the outcome." I sighed, reflecting on the last paid psychic case of my career. "Coming here has definitely made me weigh up the pros and cons of telling people I'm psychic. I have always wanted to help people, but perhaps there are better ways to do it." *There.* I wasn't admitting anything beyond errors of judgement in life choices. Any gaps that Lucien wished to fill in were down to him.

"You aren't at all what I expected," came his equally unhelpful reply. "Still…" He considered, weighing everything up in his mind.

I held my breath, knowing that the final judgement was upon me.

"I've decided that-"

"JUSSST ONE CORNETTOOOO!" the opera singer bellowed, filling the outdoor terrace - and quite possibly the entire town and its surrounding forest - with his voice.

Lucien shot me a quiet look of despair, but he'd realised that resistance was futile at some point during the first act. Instead, we settled down in the brisk autumn air and watched the show, applauding when the song came to a close.

"That was very nice," I said, doing my best to pick my words carefully. "But what happened to the second act of the frog opera?" *And the original words to that song,* I mentally added.

"Ah, well... the thing is..." The bar man blushed, turning as pink is the inside of a grapefruit. "...no one has ever let me get this far before. I never got round to writing it. But I will now, if you're going to be staying in town for a while longer?" He looked hopefully back and forth between us.

Lucien let out a noise of regret that sounded semi-believable... if you ignored the way his face was scrunched up in horror. "Unfortunately, I've got to go elsewhere. This was only a business trip for me. I wasn't even supposed to be here this long, but the local police needed my assistance."

The heck they did! I thought darkly, making a mental note to grill Lucien on how he'd pulled the wool over everyone's eyes as to his true profession. Somehow, that made me feel better about the semi-truth I was telling him, knowing that he was every bit as much of a fraud as I was.

"I would love to stay here," I said, completely honestly.

"But?" the cheerful opera singer prompted, raising his eyebrows at me.

"But... we never know what the future holds for us," I finished, and then immediately wished I'd kept my mouth closed.

"I hope you'll stay," the star of his own musical said, smiling warmly at me. He pulled out the two French sticks he'd been holding behind his back. "Please take these artisan loaves on the house. I'm hoping they'll take off, so if you like them, spread the word!" And with that, he trotted back inside, perhaps to change costume again.

"Funny. You're funny," Lucien said, apparently taking my

last comment as a joke. He pushed his chair back and shook his head, placing a note down on the table to pay for our drinks and frowning at the loaf of bread he'd been gifted. "I still don't know what to make of you, but I've decided that I don't think you're an unhinged criminal who delights in the publicity and the praise that comes from solving a case. It's a shame... that would have made an excellent documentary-length video. I'd probably have made a fortune..." His eyes glazed over as he daydreamed about the big pile of cash I could have made him if I'd been as crazy as he'd hoped.

"But you've decided?" I prompted when the daydream seemed more enticing than our conversation.

"Oh. Right. I think you're probably a genuine do-gooder. The jury is still out on your psychic powers, but... from what I've seen, you could have made a lot more money than you've been making, if you were only in it for money the way the rest of the people I expose are. Either you're really bad at business, or you help those who need it and know that nobody values anything that's free."

"It's funny how people can be, isn't it?" I agreed, before silently telling myself to tone it down. I was coming off a little too enthusiastic that I might be about to get away with my past mistakes. While I thought I'd definitely learned my lesson, I didn't want to seem too thrilled that Lucien hadn't figured out the whole truth.

"I've decided I'm going to stay for a while," he finished.

If I'd had any hot chocolate left, I'd have probably spat it out. "Why? I mean, I thought you said that you had business to be getting back to, and we've just sorted out everything between us, haven't we?"

Lucien sat back and looked at me for a long time. "Some people have found that I disappear almost like magic when the right incentive is offered. You may not have been the most nefarious businesswoman of all time, but I think you did okay."

So… that was it. Lucien Martin wanted more money.

"I'm surprised no one has outed you yet," I said dryly, thinking of the man's YouTube channel and his holier than thou attitude.

He grinned, flashing white teeth that were a favourite of many admirers in the comment section. "What can I say? Don't believe everything you see on the internet."

I sat back in my own chair and folded my arms. It was true, I probably could afford to pay Lucien Martin's price and get rid of him from my life for good. I was sure he'd cook up some baloney story about how I'd got my comeuppance to my dearly disgruntled ex-client, and I'd be free to continue the little life I was just beginning to think I might be able to make for myself here in France. All of this could be classed as a false start and forgotten about. And all I had to do was pay.

"It looks like you could be here for a while longer then," I said, making a decision of my own - that I wasn't going to feed the monster this man had become.

"Are you sure? It will give me more time to find any skeletons that are lying around the place," he warned. His voice was light, but something glinted in his eyes at the thought of a challenge.

"Let's hope you're better at looking for things than you are at hiding them," I said, standing up from the table and wrapping my scarf a little more tightly around my neck. "Maybe you'll even find time to actually contribute to the murder investigation that should be taking place right now… because even though you're pretending to be a security agent - which is a crime, by the way - I haven't seen you doing any actual police work. Plus, if you're really as good an 'investigator' as you think, you'd know that the confession the gendarmes got out of Simon Dubois is a load of nonsense!"

"I totally agree," Lucien said.

"Well, you would say that! Wait... you agree with me?" I backtracked when I realised what he'd actually said.

Lucien joined me standing up. "I do. It was obvious that Monsieur Dubois knew next to nothing about the scene of the crime. I've read the official report and he was a mile off on so many of the things he said. I should know. Figuring out when people are lying is kind of my business." He winked and I resisted the urge to wallop him over the head with the very robust French bread. The bar owner seemed to think that 'artisan' meant some sort of concrete.

"Also, I'm not actually a fake security agent. I genuinely am an international security consultant. That's my day job. I just make use of it to do my - frankly more lucrative - side hustle. Being a consultant has its benefits, like being able to pick the jobs I take on. I'm good at my job, so if there's a little more justice in the world because of me, I'll always combine the two." He smiled self-deprecatingly.

I nodded like I was buying this ridiculously humble confession of him being a man of the people. We arrived next to a wastepaper bin that was attached to a metal post in the square and I paused. "What is it you're trying to compensate for? Or make up for?" I added.

I knew I'd hit the nail on the head when a dark shadow passed across Lucien's annoyingly handsome face. "If you're really a psychic, I'm sure you already know everything you need to know," he said, shooting me an unreadable look.

I reached into my pocket and removed the spell bag I knew he'd slipped in there when he'd thought I wasn't looking, pointedly dropping it in amongst the other rubbish. Lucien's expression got even darker, before he abruptly spun on his heel and walked away, dramatically flinging his baguette in the bin as he went.

"Charming!" I muttered, still clutching my own baton. Judging by the feel of it, it would look lovely on the mantelpiece for decades to come, already having the weight and texture of a heavy piece of wood. Maybe the nameless dog would be able to tackle its crusty exterior.

The square was filling up with other locals who were bringing tables, chairs, and straw bales in preparation for the much-anticipated autumn fête tomorrow.

I waited until Lucien Martin had disappeared down one of the streets leading off the square. Then, I took the other spell bag out of the hood of my coat. "Some people never learn, no matter how many chances they're given," I said to the autumn wind, before wondering just who I was giving that advice to.

NAILED IT

The mairie was quiet when Marius and I visited it later that afternoon in search of answers. We were there to locate the letter that Sebastian Dubois alleged he'd sent to be published in the newspaper - the one that revealed the locations of his family's secret mushroom spots. I was also hoping to find out more about the guest list of the mayor's charity event because I was certain that the killer had been there that night. It was even possible that something had happened that very evening - an incident which had been the trigger for the murder of Jamie Bernard, beginning with the theft of the axe and ending with his body lying lifeless in the forest. I wanted to know everything that had happened that night.

"Did I see you having coffee with Lucien Martin earlier?" Marius asked when we were walking up a silent marble staircase.

For such a small town, the town hall was rather fancy. I wondered who'd paid for it all, and if the locals had approved of the use of their local tax money for the project. I'd heard of some towns using their annual tax for some rather eccentric things, like trips to Disneyland for the entire town. The sky was truly the limit and voting someone into office really did make a difference. I wondered what the current mayor had promised to pay for and secretly hoped it was something fun and silly. Better roads, solar panels, and infrastructure were sensible causes... but Disneyland had rides and ice cream.

"It was hot chocolate," I replied, my mind still on other things. Like Disneyland trips.

"Well, that makes *all* the difference. Did you enjoy being serenaded by the frog fanatic? Have a cosy little chat?" Marius continued in a voice laced with sarcasm.

"You're making it sound like you think I've been fraternising with the enemy," I said mildly.

Marius stopped walking when we reached a gap between floors and turned to face me.

"Was it a date, or were you discussing the case with him? I hope it was a date because you know that I am not supposed to be investigating anything. It's not my business and completely out of my hands, but if our friend from national security hears of it, I can kiss goodbye to my job. Or did you forget the reason he's in town?"

Strangely enough, I hadn't thought about what the cover story Lucien had told meant for the police in Sellenoise because I'd been operating under the assumption that Lucien was a complete fake and that there would be no final report on their police work. With Lucien claiming he really was who he purported to be, Marius had a point about me keeping my mouth shut... and I may have already committed a faux pas. I wracked my brains, trying to remember every detail of my conversation with Lucien, sifting through the things I'd focused on in the heat of the moment and looking for anything that might get my partner in solving crime into trouble. I thought that Lucien at least suspected that we were investigating the very thing we were not supposed to be investigating, but what he was going to do about it - if anything - remained an unanswered question. I felt a pang of guilt, knowing that I could have handed over some cash today and saved Marius from this stressful situation.

"I'm sure everything will work out for the best," I said, settling for blind optimism in the face of doubt.

"Is that a psychic prediction, or just an inane saying that means nothing at all?"

This time, I kept my lips firmly buttoned until we reached the claret red door of an office, which featured a silver-coloured plaque that bore the French word for mayor. Below it was a plastic tag reading Gabriel Sevres that slid into an interchangeable slot and below that was another name - Selena Indre.

"Let's hope Selena is working this afternoon," Marius said, adjusting his collar, so that it was lying perfectly flat, and patting his hair down. I kept my raised eyebrows to myself when he knocked on the door and immediately entered without waiting for an answer. Something told me that Marius had been watching Lucien's abrupt behaviour and was hoping he'd see similar results.

A woman with dyed blonde hair in a high bun with a pretty silken scarf wrapped around her head and tied above her hairline spun around in her chair in surprise at Marius' sudden entrance. She muttered a rude word when she realised that she'd knocked over the jar of deep pink nail polish she'd been touching up her false nails with when we'd made our sudden entrance into the room.

"I was just on my break," she explained, obviously flustered at being caught out. "I'll just be a second... uh..." She turned back to the computer screen, which was angled enough for me to see it. The mayor's secretary quickly minimised the racy story website she'd been on. I caught a glimpse of her inbox whilst she was cursing under her breath at the polish now smudging the keyboard, clicking her left hand on the mouse ferociously as she tried to get the computer to respond.

I wondered if the mayor was taking any public action over the death of one of his residents, but there was nothing in the inbox that jumped out at me immediately. All I saw was a mixture of personal and professional subjects, including *OLAF urgent call, PIERRE pumpkin problem,* and *Council meeting agenda.*

"That's a great colour," I said to Selena, who immediately stopped the flurry of action and beamed at me.

"Thanks! I love all things pink."

"Me too!" I said, waving my own nails at her.

Marius cleared his throat, causing us both to stare at him. "I... do not like pink..." he strangely decided to clarify before continuing with: "I'm here on a police matter. We need information because of... a police matter," he repeated.

I realised that - yet again - we'd come here in such a rush that no cover story had been created for why we might need to see a charity event guest list and a letter that may or may not exist without it having anything to do with the theoretically solved murder of Jamie Bernard. Fortunately, coming up with stories on the spur of the moment was one of my talents. It wasn't one I liked to use often, but I was undeniably good at it. Things like that were easy when you could figure out a lot of things about a person just by looking at them and their surroundings. Creating a believable fiction tailored to them was just a matter of taking it one step further.

"You've probably heard I'm starting my new therapy business in town," I said, knowing when it was time to take over from the floundering policeman. "I was chatting to Damien Rue about it, and he thinks the best way to start things off with a bang is to throw a party at his house. This is a little embarrassing, but as I don't know many people in town yet, he thought it might be an idea to start with the same group of people who came to his house for the last party he threw. I'm not sure if any of them would want to come, but I've heard that the mayor is a big supporter of local businesses, so fingers crossed! Do you happen to have an old guest list lying around? Damien's mislaid his copy and thought you might have one."

The secretary looked at me for long enough that I thought I was about to be called out, but her mouth curved up into another smile and I nearly sighed with relief. She was on my side.

"No problemo! I can look that up for you, but what was the police matter that was so important to you, Marius?" For just a second, something nervous flitted across Selena's expression.

Marius' face went slack for a moment. "Oh, it was just that…"

"We're actually here for another reason as well as the guest list," I interrupted, hoping Marius would forgive me for it. I knew when someone was trying to think on their feet, and Marius seemed more likely to fall on his face. "A therapy client of mine sent a letter anonymously to the town's news-paper. I believe it's due to be published in the next issue. After due consideration, the sender of the letter would like to withdraw it, and in the interests of anonymity, I've been sent to collect it. The reason this is a police matter concerns the contents of the aforementioned letter. Did you happen to open it already?"

"I think I know the one you're talking about," Selena said, looking curious but trying to conceal it. "It arrived a couple of weeks ago, and it said it should only be opened on the day the paper was finalised this week and was due to be sent to print, but… I'm afraid I looked at it as soon as it arrived. I couldn't resist." She turned and batted her eyelids at Marius, who turned a remarkable shade of pink. "Does that mean I'm in some sort of trouble with the police?"

"No, not at all," he replied, pushing his hair back self-consciously. "Precisely when did it arrive? And did you happen to see what it contained?"

Selena blinked. "Of course I saw what it contained. Why else would I have opened it?" She followed it up with a smile that made Marius gaze pointedly at the books on the shelf behind her as he tried to stop being so tongue-tied. I wasn't sure whether I should be the bearer of the bad news that it wasn't just Lucien's shiny new factor that made him a hit with the ladies. For all his faults, he was good at talking to people and had a kind of charisma that couldn't be learned. Marius went to pieces whenever he was around someone he liked.

Selena fluffed her bun up, making it even more fashion-ably messy. "The letter was a list of locations for mushroom picking. It gave the varieties and the seasons when you should visit and included a handy map that was also supposed to be published. I thought it was rather fun. I was intrigued as to who might share something like this, and if it's even the real deal. I was actually debating whether to publish or not, knowing the stir it could cause. Especially after the recent drama involving mushrooms in the town." She looked between us at our blank faces. "When our local mushroom seller was hauled off for confessing to murder?" she prompted.

I frowned, having almost forgotten about the murder confession while Marius and I had barrelled our way towards what we hoped was the real truth about what had happened to Jamie Bernard.

"The letter actually arrived here on the day of the mayor's

charity event. Weird coincidence, right?" She smiled dreamily. "I put it in the folder with the other letters for publication in future issues. Once I've published them, they get put into a different file. Pretty organised, isn't it? Before I arrived, the paper was a mess - a total disaster! Honestly, the mayor is lucky he has me around. Next election, he should definitely give me some sort of credit." A line creased her forehead for a moment before it relaxed again as she shook away whatever thought had just crossed her mind. "Anyway, I can get it for you right now. Was there anything else?" she asked, reaching across the desk and fumbling around for a bright yellow folder.

"Is there a possibility that anyone else might have already seen that letter?" Marius asked, none too subtly.

Selena's hand froze on the way to the folder. I could almost hear the cogs turning in her head. "Well, the mayor sometimes takes the folder home with him to check things through. Also, quite a few people come through this office to see the mayor. He's very good at talking to locals about their concerns, no matter what some in town say about him," she said defensively, making me wonder when she'd assumed we were accusing the mayor of something.

Something like having access to the letter! my brain pinged and I filed it away for later consideration.

"I put the letter back in the envelope it came in. I doubt anyone else has opened it since. Let me just find it…"

While she rifled through the folder filled with lined paper and hand scrawled messages, I glanced at the secretary's desk. As well as spare fake nails, nail polish, and a file, she had a row of neat miniature jam jars filled with office supplies. A photo showed a picture of a well-fed cat looking pretty resentful about being dressed up in a top hat and frilly collar. Next to it was a calendar with the boxes filled with appointments. I noted that this secretary went above and beyond with a weekly date to order in the mayor's takeaway on Friday night and briefing meetings with him on Thursday evenings, with a smattering of other engagements written in over the month involving various local institutions. I switched my attention back to Selena, who was waving a dog-eared envelope with an air of triumph.

"Here we go! You can see where I opened it and then stuck it back down." She tilted her head, clearly wondering if anyone else had seen the inside of the letter, but she shrugged a second later, unsure of what to think. Combined with the inauspicious timing of the letter's arrival, the ins and outs of the mairie on the day of the mayor's charity party could hold the key to unravelling the case. It all depended upon the contents of the letter.

Marius wasted no time opening it and pulled out the piece of paper within, his eyes scanning it for several seconds. He didn't say anything but his eyes found mine and I knew.

The site where Jamie Bernard had met his end was no coincidence. He'd been killed at one of the Dubois family's secret mushroom spots... and the information on how to find that place had arrived right before the night the axe had gone missing from Damien Rue's house.

The door to the office swung open and Maia Sevres entered without knocking. She hesitated for a second when she saw us standing there, but her surprise instantly turned to a smile of welcome.

"Hello again, Justine. I'm glad to see you're already making friends in town," she said, sparkling towards Marius.

Marius made a small sound that I knew was him resisting the urge to deny that anything was going on between us and affirm that this was totally professional, whilst knowing he couldn't say anything that might suggest he was investigating something he wasn't supposed to be looking into. The mayor's wife knowing the truth was the same as the mayor knowing… and the mayor knowing meant that the next pair of ears to hear that truth would undoubtedly be the pair that belonged to Monsieur Duval, who was presumably at home taking a long bath to get rid of all the pig mud.

"Everyone has been very friendly," I agreed as mildly as I could to spare Marius from any gossip.

"Marius showed her the way here," Selena contributed, surprising me by telling a lie on our behalf. Perhaps there was hope for Marius' obvious affection being returned after all.

I reached out and took the piece of paper that Selena had just printed. "I'm afraid I have to get back to work. Everyone has been very encouraging about the therapy I'm offering. My door is always open if there's ever anything you'd like to come and chat about," I added, knowing I was probably pushing my luck… but every opportunity not taken was an opportunity missed.

"I may do that. Or you could come to me for that cup of tea," Maia said, subtly suggesting that her place was infinitely better than mine. To be honest, it probably was.

"Lovely!" I said, nodding at her and Selena before trotting back out of the office with Marius following, hoping that we'd managed to complete our mission without too much scrutiny or gossip being started.

"Selena, is my husband around?" I heard Maia ask as the door was swinging shut behind us.

"I'm not sure. He's been in and out all day because of the fête organising."

"You mean you don't know if your employer is in his office right now? Isn't that your job?"

The door shut, muting any response that Selena might have given.

Marius shook his head as we descended the stairs. "Selena's main job is keeping Maia happy. Just between us, I think that's why Gabriel employed her in the first place - to handle his wife. Prior to him taking office, the position of secretary was usually taken by one of the retirees in town because it was considered to be a very part time position. Gabriel has changed that, but he's also taken a much more active role in the town's affairs. On the whole, I think it's approved of, even with the additional budget. The way I hear it, most are happy with the current mayor, but if you try to change anything around here you'll meet resistance. That's just how it is. Places like Sellenoise view progress as a disease, not a cure."

"What do we do now?" I wondered when we reached the bottom of the stairs and waited, looking out at the strings of lights that were being turned on to test them. They bobbed merrily in the cold breeze that blew across the square. I hoped that the marquees had been well anchored and that all livestock had shelters to stay warm in the cold night to come.

Marius reached out and I handed him the guest list, glancing at it first and taking a mental picture of the names written there. It looked like half the town had been present at this charity event. I immediately accepted it would take more than a guest list and a mushroom map to work out both the motive for the murder and the mastermind behind it. "How come you didn't go to this event?" I asked, not seeing Marius' name on the list.

"Well, I was…" He considered coming up with an excuse but sighed, his on the spot thinking failing him again. "I had a date out of town that night. I was hoping that going out with someone who hasn't known me their whole life might be a good thing."

I nodded sympathetically and he glared at me for assuming that the date had gone badly, even though we both knew it had.

Marius cleared his throat "I wonder if Selena told anyone else about the letter when it arrived and she opened it?" He glanced at the guest list himself and also didn't spot any smoking guns. Or in this case... axe murderers.

"You mean the mayor?" I prompted, thinking along the same lines as Marius. Something like the mushroom map would be the hottest gossip in town when it was released. It was difficult to see Selena keeping it a secret. I was actually impressed that the map hadn't escaped far earlier than intended.

"Damien did say that Jamie Bernard was spotted bothering him on the night of his own charity event. Perhaps we should find out what that conversation was about. It seems that everyone had a bone to pick with Jamie Bernard. I wonder what he had on the mayor?"

"I do think something happened at that party. Jamie pushed someone over the edge that night, and we need to find out what line he crossed." I sighed and looked out across the square. It was a festive juxtaposition in the face of the terrible crime that had been committed so recently. Somehow, it just drove home how certain people, who had done things that had made them unloved in life, remained that way in death. The message was clear - some people were better forgotten. I felt a stab of worry that it was a fate that could happen to anyone. *It's your good deeds that matter in life, not being remembered for them,* I reminded myself, the cool voice of reason in my head taking over. Wanting to be remembered was a strange kind of desperation. Instead, the focus should be on putting as much good into the world as possible because, remembered or not, a little bit of good was like a seed that grew and flourished. A memory was merely a snapshot.

"Are you going to the fête tomorrow?" I asked Marius, before wondering why I'd asked such a stupid question. Sellenoise was so small and quiet everyone who could make it out of their house would be there.

"I'll be working as usual. Someone has to keep things in order around here, and it certainly won't be Monsieur Duval. He always books this day off, so he can spend all day by the wine stall." He rubbed his chin reflexively. "Although, after today's events, maybe he won't be so keen." He shrugged his shoulders. "It's always a busy day. You'd be amazed at how many of the old dears around here are light fingered. They only ever get a slap on the wrist. No one thinks it's a good idea to saddle grandmas and grandads with criminal records, but you'd be shocked at the items they manage to get their mitts on and the places they conceal them."

I looked sideways at Marius, somehow thinking that this was one of those times when being specific would have been better than being vague. Imagination was probably worse than the reality.

"Thank goodness Sellenoise has you to keep everyone safe," I said, my tongue firmly pressed into my cheek.

Marius puffed out his chest. "I'm just doing my duty," he replied, taking me entirely seriously.

I kept my smile to myself, wondering if that sort of thing simply didn't translate from English to French. It was that or Marius didn't have much experience of someone pulling his leg. He would learn very fast if he spent more time with me.

"I'll let you know if I think of anything else about the case we're not investigating," I said, winking at him.

"Yes, uh... definitely do that," he replied, looking every bit as uncomfortable as he had done in the office with the secretary.

"I should be getting back to the station in case anything's happened," he announced, pulling himself up to his full height and doing his best to look professional and detached.

I watched him walk across the square, nodding and

greeting the last few setters-up in the fading light. Even though Marius wondered why he didn't attract the same kind of attention that Lucien Martin absorbed like a sponge, Sellenoise loved him, and that was worth more than all the charisma in the world.

* * *

The dog and I enjoyed our walk that evening. The streets were silent as the chill crept in, reminding everyone that winter was already spreading its icy claws, stealing the warmth from the earth that the summer before had imbued it with.

Thoughts swirled around in my head like the leaves blown into town from the forest, but nothing stuck out to me. It was a good thing I'd dropped the whole psychic act. Right now, I'd be reduced to telling people that the future was shrouded in fog... try again later - like a cheap mechanical fortuneteller at a fair. I sighed as we walked back towards home, just two outsiders in a town that had more secrets than I could shake a stick at. I wondered when the truth would come out.

The dog pulled on the lead when a black cat darted across the road, skittering away into the night. He turned back and looked at me, as if to ask why cats were so fast and he was banned from chasing them. I answered him with a stern look and a call to return to me. When the dog obeyed, I stroked his ginger and white head, wondering who had been his owner before, and what had gone so terribly wrong.

"It's you and me now," I said, knowing that it was true. "And I think it's time for a name."

The dog sat down and tilted his head at me, almost as if he was waiting to judge what I came up with. My eyes searched the street, hunting for divine inspiration. I'd never had to name anything before. Somehow, it suddenly seemed incredibly important.

"What about... Leaf?" I suggested. The dog whined. "You're right, that's not a great start. Baguette?" I tried and was met with a disbelieving look.

We walked on for a bit in a contemplative silence. Just as we were making the turn back into the street where we lived, a light came on in a porch and the warm glow of electricity illuminated the perfect orange globe that sat on the doormat of the intended recipient of an unusual gift - judging by the bow it had been tied with.

"Pumpkin," I said, naming the autumnal vegetable out loud and then glancing at the dog. He just shot me another look and pulled onwards. According to him, I was rubbish at this naming thing.

We arrived home and I reflected how welcome the little light I'd left on in the sitting room looked through the pane of glass as the wind rattled on through. It would be even better once I'd got a fire going and settled in for the night with my cute and cuddly company.

I was about to open the door when I noticed there was something hanging from the handle. My mind immediately jumped to Lucien Martin. I wondered what dirty trick this was, before I realised there was a label attached and a message written in handwriting that definitely didn't belong to my current adversary.

I gently lifted the bundle off the handle and read the note.

I noticed you love tea and thought you might enjoy this blend of chai tea spices. All you need to do is put it in an infuser and leave it in hot water for three minutes, or longer if you want to spice things up. You can't see as much as with tea leaves, but sometimes taste is better than sight!

Marissa xxx

I held up the bag and my nose was filled with the scent of cinnamon, cloves, ginger, and black tea. "The spice is right," I joked to the dog, who yipped in response. "Look at you, laughing at my bad jokes! You know the way into my heart."

The dog yipped again. I looked down at his happy canine face that seemed to be smiling at me.

"Spice?" I suggested and heard another yip. "I'll take that as a yes. Spice it is!" And just like that, the perfect name for my pet dog presented itself and the first feeling of *home* wrapped around me and whispered that I could stay here forever. All I needed to do was nudge this one little investigation in the right direction, and then Sellenoise could return to being a place where nothing ever happened. I could settle down and solve problems I was actually qualified to solve.

It sounded so easy standing in the doorway of the little stone cottage with a gift of tea in my hand and the warmth of the town's togetherness in my heart. I should have known that life never missed a chance to throw a curve ball whenever the sailing looked a little too smooth.

The fire started easily. I thought I caught a nasty whiff of whatever had been in the little bags of nonsense that Lucien had left in my house, but it was soon gone and replaced with just a hint of woodsmoke, before the flames took over. Everything rushed away up the chimney and out into the night, where it mingled with countless other fires being burned, as the people of Sellenoise sought to keep the cold at bay.

"I think I should try some of that tea, Spice," I said to the newly named dog, who wagged his tail in response.

A smile danced on my lips as we went to the kitchen together. While the tea brewed, I gave him pieces of apple, which he devoured as if he hadn't been fed for a year. I knew it would probably take time to improve his relationship with food after what he must have been through, but time was a great healer for all wounds, and time was something I thought there was probably plenty of in Sellenoise.

Just so long as I figured out a way to see the back of Lucien Martin.

I pushed around the infuser and inhaled the scent of the tea, hoping that inspiration would strike twice in one night. The sound of something scraping upstairs wasn't the sign from above I was hoping for.

It had sounded as though someone was trying to open a window.

Ice flowed through my veins and I froze on the spot, forgetting about the tea I'd just brewed. Spice and I exchanged a look.

"That's either someone breaking in... or someone trying to leave," I said in a low voice. "Neither of those options is good."

13

ARTISANAL ATTACK

Spice whined but stayed by my side, looking questioningly at me, as if to say: 'You're going to fix it, right?'.

I raised an eyebrow at him. "Some guard dog you make!"

We tiptoed out into the main room. The fire had died down from the lack of attention whilst I'd been making the tea. The dim glow cast dark shadows in the corners of the room that danced with the fading flames, as if there were monsters lurking everywhere I looked. I nearly jumped out of my skin when something bumped against my leg.

"Oh! Good thinking," I said to Spice, who had something in his mouth that he dropped as soon as I reached for it. I lifted up the rock solid artisan bread that Julien had given to me as a thank you for listening to his opera. Having a weapon to hand might be a good idea, and this definitely qualified as one.

Armed with an ancient baguette and a dog who would probably be out of the door at the first sign of trouble, we ventured up the stairs.

The cold air that blew on my face was the first sign that

something was really wrong. I held my breath and listened, but even with Spice as silent as a ghost by my side, there wasn't a single sound beyond the crackling of the fire. Either the danger had passed... or the person breaking in, or trying to leave, was doing the same thing as I was right now.

The hairs rising on the back of my neck warned me not to let my guard down.

A sudden courage seized me - probably caused by adrenaline being pumped around my body - but I continued on my way up the stairs with my grip tight around the baguette. Lucien Martin clearly thought he could scare me into falling for whatever ridiculous internet exposé he was surely still planning. I could already tell he was a sore loser, but messing with someone's home was crossing a line, and I intended to utilise my baguette in a very artisanal way to express my opinion.

With all of the finesse of a ninja who enjoyed more cake than the average ninja, I leaped into the open plan upstairs of the cottage with my baguette raised high. In truth, I'd half convinced myself that all of this was in my head - the product of a day spent facing off against a cunning killer and an annoying adversary, culminating in paranoia that was surely nothing more than an errant blast of wind combined with a rather elderly building. All of that made seeing the outline of a man silhouetted against the window at the far end of the room even more terrifying.

For a second, I froze up again, all ninja-like bravery deserting me in the face of the horrifying unknown. Out of the corner of my eye, I saw Spice slip back downstairs to where it was safe and warm.

I was on my own.

But I could do this.

That was what I told myself, channelling all of the determination and positivity I always tried to pass on to my clients into myself. A lot of people found themselves in situations beyond their control, facing things they'd never faced before, and they triumphed against the odds.

Playing to your strengths was the key to surviving these situations, and my strength was seeing things that others missed. Things like the fact that the position of the feet on the carpet showed that this man had his back turned, and even as I continued to stand with my baguette thrust out in front of me, he bent down to do something to the shelves below the window. *Probably thinks he can hide more of his nasty little bags, or worse!* I thought, anger replacing the anxiety as I took advantage of the intruder's distracted state and rushed forward.

"IS THIS PSYCHIC ENOUGH FOR YOU?!" I yelled as I delivered a stunning blow with the stick of bread to the back of the crouching man's neck. He collapsed forwards with a muffled yell, the shelves coming off the wall as he fell, struck down by my artisanal attack from above. "How dare you break in to my house?"

"I was just fixing the shelves!" the man on the floor replied.

"That's a terrible excuse!" I scoffed, before realising that it genuinely *would* be a terrible excuse... if the man I'd just hit was Lucien Martin.

With a sudden feeling of uncertainty, I trotted over to the light switch by the bed and turned it on.

The man lying on the floor was not Lucien Martin, but I did recognise him.

I'd just attacked my landlord, Pierre.

"What did you hit me with?" he asked, rubbing his neck and twisting his head back and forth, as if it could possibly be broken. He eyed the object in my hand. "That looks like one of Julien's loaves. The man has a thing about crusty bread. Somehow, he's managed to make bread that consists of only the crust. Heaven help us all if he ever turned his mind to something truly evil. Why did you hit me?!"

"I thought you were breaking in! Why are you inside the house?" I replied, my guilt at attacking my landlord over-come by the need to know why he was inside the rented accommodation without permission under the pretence of fixing a shelf at a fairly late hour of the night.

Pierre opened his mouth to answer the question but was interrupted by a loud hammering on the door. Downstairs, Spice barked twice. I turned away from my strange landlord and went back down, wary of the entire street being woken up.

The banging came again. I opened the door and nearly received a fist to the face as the person on the other side tried to knock once more.

"Justine! Thank goodness you're okay. I think there's an intruder in your house," she announced, stepping past me and pulling a collapsible umbrella out of her pocket in such a practiced way, I sensed this wasn't the first time she'd used it as a weapon.

"How did you know?" I asked.

"He's upstairs. The two of us should be able to handle him," she replied, stalking onwards with Spice wagging his tail and following her like this was a fun new game. "I was walking past and I saw you downstairs and a shadow upstairs. I guess I've just got a sixth sense about these things, but I could tell he wasn't supposed to be there. Why else would he have been in the dark?"

"No need to use the umbrella, I confronted him right before you knocked on the door," I told her - albeit reluctantly.

"Oh," Marissa said, looking rather deflated that there wasn't a call for an umbrella being used for an alternative purpose. "Did you take him out? Is there a body that needs hiding?" she added in an undertone.

"No... I..." I hesitated when it occurred to me that Marissa hadn't sounded like her first port of call would be the police in a situation like that. Perhaps I needed to watch the people of Sellenoise a little more carefully. "...I hit him with a baguette," I said, glancing back towards the stairs and wondering what Pierre was doing right now. And what he'd been doing here in the first place. "I feel bad about it now. There's probably an explanation."

"I doubt it will be a reasonable one," Marissa said, her grip not loosening on the umbrella. "Pierre has a reputation for this sort of thing around here. There's a reason why your cottage was vacant."

"I had noticed he enjoyed peeping. I put a stop to that though," I said, thinking of the filler I'd utilised when I'd moved in.

"I think I'd like to hear his explanation as to why he is here. You didn't invite him, did you?" she added, wanting to make absolutely certain of the situation.

I shook my head and let her lead the way, curious about what her intentions were. I thought Pierre might be about to be given a flea in his ear to go with the crusty breadcrumbs.

"Explain yourself!" Marissa demanded when we made it to the top of the stairs.

Pierre took one look at the local postmistress and tried to leave the property via the window.

"You've pried for the last time!" Marissa yelled, her umbrella work second to none as the sheepish landlord tried to fend off blows with a book taken from the shelf. He sensibly surrendered.

"I was fixing shelves!" he tried again, but Marissa shot him such a murderous look that he gulped visibly. "I really was! I was *going* to fix them..."

"And no doubt add a camera or something else creepy at the same time? Or were you planning to hide under the bed? Pierre, you've done this before and I told you then that the police would be involved if this ever happened again. You're lucky we don't sling you into the river!"

"I wasn't doing anything wrong. It's my property... and she's got a dog!" he replied, trying to claw back some points in his favour. "That was not in the agreement and I'm not okay with it. Maybe I was coming to see if she had a dog in here."

"Then you should have started with that excuse. I might have bought it for two seconds longer than your shelf fixing sham," Marissa said, cutting my landlord down quicker than a lumberjack in a tree cutting contest.

Pierre stuck his bottom lip out and looked surly, muttering something about this being his property and he was allowed to make the rules anyway he saw fit. Marissa cut him off in the middle of his little speech.

"No you don't! You were warned and you swore you would change your ways. It's not up to Eloise to keep you in line. I would have thought that a man of your age would know better by now. Shame on you!" Marissa turned back to me. "If I were you, I'd be looking for a new property to stay in. I know plenty of people who could rent you a room until you get sorted, although admittedly, entire properties to rent are rare around here. Houses get bought or passed down through families. The rental market isn't exactly booming because..." She spread her arms wide. "...why would anyone rent when they spend their whole lives here? But you do have your business to think about," she acknowledged.

"I also gave no permission for this house to be used as a business premises," Pierre complained. "I want more money for both things!"

Marissa looked at me for a long moment, like a judge

passing a sentence after weighing up the evidence in front of her. "Here's what's going to happen," she announced. "If Justine wants to stay here after the gross invasion of privacy you just inflicted upon her in a place she rented from you in good faith, then there will be conditions attached."

"Good!" Pierre said, jumping the gun.

"Because of what you've done, and what I'm sure you've been doing all along..." Here, Marissa looked pointedly towards the wall that the cottage shared with Pierre's cottage next door, and I thought again of the gaps I'd 'fixed' as soon as I'd moved in. "...a penalty amount will be deducted from the rent you are charging Justine. In order to run her business and be permitted to keep her very well behaved dog here, who she so clearly shares a magical bond with, she will pay you extra rent to cover it - let's say... equal to that of the penalty you've just conceded for being a creep." Marissa nodded once, the matter apparently decided.

"Why would I agree to that?" Pierre groused, looking unhappily from the umbrella to the baguette that I was still holding for some reason.

"Because otherwise, you've missed your final chance to not be ousted from the community. Pierre, we both know this isn't the first time, but it's going to be the last. Now... deal or no deal, as they say on television?" Marissa finished. I wondered why she'd become a postmistress when it was obvious that she would do equally well in a boardroom full of executives, cutting her competitors down to size. This woman knew the art of a deal.

"Fine," Pierre said after much unintelligible grumbling.

"And no more interfering, or the same consequences apply." Marissa clapped her hands together. "Excellent! Pierre... get out - using the stairs!" she added when my landlord turned back to face the window.

The three of us and Spice walked back down the stairs

and Pierre was escorted to the door of a house he owned, before being booted out onto the street.

"There! That wasn't so bad, was it?" Marissa said. "You get better terms, and Pierre gets something to think about. Somehow, I think this might be the turning point for him. The dent on that baguette would certainly suggest he'll have something to think about for the next week of so."

I lifted the bread in question and realised that Marissa was right. There was a significant indent in the side of what Pierre had called solid crust.

"Don't try toasting that. It doesn't improve it. In fact, it makes what was previously hard turn into something even more solid, which you honestly wouldn't believe was possible. I don't know what Julien puts in his loaves. Several people hang their bread gifts on the wall, or use them as doorstops. Sometimes, I wonder if Julien isn't having us all on with his bad bread and strange musical taste. He probably goes home at night and butters some of the best bread ever baked in town, puts on a CD of smooth jazz, and laughs at us all."

I considered Marissa's theory. "Why did you go with smooth jazz as the antithesis to opera?"

Marissa rubbed her chin in thought, adjusting the bright orange scarf she had tied around her neck at a jaunty angle. "I'm not actually sure. Perhaps that assumption reveals something meaningful about me." She looked at me in a curious way that was very familiar. Clients often thought that small innocuous decisions or ideas they'd expressed would reveal something important about themselves without them realising it.

"Thank you for coming to my rescue. I'm not sure what I was thinking, attacking an intruder with some bread. In all honesty, I wasn't expecting it to be Pierre," I said, hoping to draw a line under the events of this evening.

"Was there someone in particular you *were* expecting to enter your house through an upstairs window?" Marissa asked, her eyes sparkling with speculative thoughts.

"I suppose logically, no... although, I'm actually curious how Pierre managed to come in that way when he didn't have a ladder." He hadn't been in the house when I'd come back with Spice, of that much I was certain. Pierre was not a man who moved quietly with ease, and I also trusted Spice's ears far more than my own. They'd pricked up at the sound of the window opening when before he'd been perfectly at ease.

"It's actually quite easy to explain..." Marissa began but the answer had already occurred to me.

"The roof..." I said before she could continue.

A smile spread across her lips and she nodded at me, encouraging me to continue.

"The ceiling upstairs doesn't reflect the shape of the roof outside. This cottage is attached to the one next door where Pierre lives. I presume the two attics are connected, probably because once upon a time, these houses were barns and then later converted. Plus, there's a hayloft door at the top of the house." I rubbed my chin. "So, what I heard would've been Pierre coming out of the hayloft above and then in through the outside window." I frowned. "It seems incredibly dangerous for something that hardly seems worth it."

"Don't put anything past a man like Pierre," Marissa said with a thin-lipped smile.

I bit my lip in concern. I'd guessed Pierre's nature when I'd moved in, but this was an oversight I was stunned that I'd missed. It was so unlike me. Was I off my game? What other glaringly obvious things had I neglected to notice? A chill ran through me at the thought of the murderer's identity being practically signed on the body in the forest and me somehow missing it.

I took a deep breath, reminding myself that, as I wasn't psychic or magically gifted with powers from an invisible force, there was no 'losing' my ability. Instead, I'd been tired, overworked, and focusing on other problems. Something had slipped me by, but getting hung up on it would only make me miss other important observations in the present.

"I'm impressed," Marissa said, folding her arms and casually leaning against the wall in the small entrance hall.

"I'm not," I replied, admittedly still a little hung up on what had happened.

Marissa made a sound of amusement. "I should apologise. Pierre's a pest, but we all thought he was being watched closely enough and under threat of serious consequences, should he do anything weird. I do hope it won't put you off our town, and if you do want to move out, I could probably pull some strings."

I considered, weighing up my options. "I think I'll stay here for now. You've got me a good deal, and the reason Pierre broke in here was because I'd already foiled his other little games," I concluded, considering the evidence and seeing this as a desperate attempt. Pierre was someone whose behaviour was quite easy to predict when you were aware of his nature. The only reason I hadn't seen it coming was because I'd been thinking about others whose true natures remained a mystery to me. If I'd had my eyes open, the truth would have been in plain sight all along.

"I'm glad of it. This is a good place to start your search for something more permanent. Don't tell me you're not thinking of buying and settling down. I know when someone is staying here for good, and you've got that look about you. I think you'll do just fine here." Marissa smiled. "I should probably get going and leave you to a quieter evening with your dog. If there's ever anything you need, I'm always around, and you'll always have the benefit of my umbrella any day."

"The same goes for you... except you'll have my baguette," I replied equally sincerely.

We smiled at one another, both knowing that the seeds of friendship that had been sown the first time we'd met when she'd come to visit for tea were already starting to sprout. I also knew that Marissa had done more for me than tonight's dramatic defence, and that was something I wanted to settle.

"Night!" she said, raising a hand and opening the door to leave.

I took a breath, knowing it was now or never. "I must thank you for the chai tea you left for me, but I think I should also be thanking you for the plant cuttings you left on my car and around my windows. They were intended to be a gift, weren't they?"

Marissa hesitated in the doorway, her face still angled towards the night beyond. "It was intended to help you," she finished, answering my question the way I'd suspected it would be answered.

"I thought so," I told her with a smile that I hoped would convey that we were still on good terms and that this hadn't been an interrogation.

"Good," Marissa replied, her shoulders relaxing. "Sometimes people see things in a different way. I shouldn't have done it so secretively, but I wasn't sure." She smiled apologetically, before her expression sobered again. "I meant what I said about being wary of the stranger. Something tells me his business in this town is not finished. Rather like that murder investigation I think you're working on with a certain local policeman."

I opened my mouth to say otherwise, thinking of Marius' job, but Marissa would smell a lie, and I also sensed that she wasn't going to be whispering into the ear of Monsieur

Duval - whom she undoubtedly thought dimly of. "I'm keeping an eye on it," I said, knowing it would be enough to reassure her.

"I thought you probably were. When I sent that note, I was still getting your measure. Now, I would certainly look at it in a different light. I think I'd even question who should beware of the other. Maybe I sent the note to the wrong person," she said, her eyes sparkling. "But, we can never be quite sure of the identities of people from the first things they reveal about themselves. What lies inside can be quite different from what's on the outside. I'm never surprised when I'm surprised. Have a good evening... and maybe lock that window from the inside."

"I certainly will," I reassured her, lifting my hand in farewell when she went out into the night.

I was still smiling about Marissa's thoughts on people's insides being different from their outsides when something pinged in my mind. It related to outsides not always reflecting what lay within.

I mentally ran through all I'd seen on the secretary's computer screen today. I'd assumed that she'd been clicking to cover up the questionable story site she'd been reading, but she'd continued clicking even after it had minimised, hadn't she?

As if she'd wanted to hide something else that had been visible on screen.

Like the subject of an email.

"Olaf is not a typical French name," I muttered, picking up on the the only subject line that seemed strange.

It was with my heart beating faster than normal that I Googled the innocuous name written in capitals and opened up a brand new can of worms.

14

PHONEYS AND FRAUDS

I t's funny how when the answer is finally in front of you it all seems so obvious. I'd always wondered why our brains are hardwired to scream that at us when something becomes clear for the first time. When you already have the answer, of course it all makes sense. That doesn't alter the fact that before the blinding light of illumination shone down, the fog of uncertainty was genuinely thick, so why are revelations so often accompanied by the sensation of kicking oneself?

"Don't jump to conclusions yet," I said the next morning when I pulled out my mobile phone, checked the opening hours online, and made the call I needed to make to confirm my suspicions. I only hoped I could convince the person on the other end of the phone line to tell me far more than I had a right to know. It was time to put myself to the test against a psychological opponent.

I took two deep breaths when I heard the phone ring on the other end of the line. There was a small click as it was answered and I began what I hoped would be just enough deceit to justify reaching the truth. A killer lived among the residents of Sellenoise, and I might be on the cusp of finding the motive that had driven them to kill.

"I'm a national security agent calling about a case you have open for a town called Sellenoise." I focused my attention on keeping my voice low - masculine without sounding false. I hoped it was convincing enough because I was about to play my first card. "I'm seeking an update on an incident of fraud relating to some EU funding."

There was a small pause on the other end of the line. I counted the seconds, wondering if I'd been caught already by something I'd said. I was good at reading people, but it was so much harder when you couldn't see their face.

"What's your name, please?" the voice on the other end of the line came back.

I shut my eyes.

I'd known this moment would come.

Not even the most confident caller would get away with asking for information from the European Anti-Fraud Office (OLAF for short) on a case that was most likely confidential without at least giving their name. I was already at the stage where I needed to play the ace up my sleeve. Whether I won or went bust relied on the truth having been told by another person.

"Lucien Martin," I said, feeling everything hang in the balance.

There was another silence. I sensed the woman was checking my credentials. I was relying on Lucien having told me the truth about his role as a genuine national security agent. Even if there was a record of him, there would probably be further credentials I'd have to share in order to prove myself. And those were credentials I didn't know.

Which was why this next part required some acting.

"I must stress how urgent this is. I am in town investigating a murder and we have reason to believe that this incident forms part of the motive. Gabriel Sevres instructed me to call you directly. He spoke of how helpful you've been in working to resolve the matter, which is why he thought you'd be able to summarise the key points and progress for me as succinctly and accurately as possible. The prime suspect is due to be released in just six hours' time, if further evidence has not been presented. I do not say this lightly, but every minute counts." I pulled a face when I'd finished, wondering if that had been a little too cinematic for its own good. Life was generally a lot more mundane than drama on screen. I'd written down the rough script, noting in advance the direction the conversation would take, but I'd definitely improvised from the original plan, and it was an entirely different matter to see words written down and then hear them come out of your own mouth in a voice you were trying to maintain at an octave lower than normal.

It was probably totally transparent.

If I was lucky, I'd get away with this being considered a prank call.

If I was unlucky, the consequences would be much, much worse.

Lucien Martin wouldn't have to worry about proving me to be a psychic fraud. He'd have proof I was the regular kind of fraud, too.

"Sorry for the delay, Monsieur Martin. It took me a moment to find the Sellenoise file. According to this, the 100,000 euros of EU funding fraudulently taken by email from the offices of the local mairie remains an open case. The scammers have not yet been located, although it is suspected that they are a group who have tried the same techniques with many small towns in receipt of such funding. They often succeed, if truth be told."

I pushed down my surprise at having been believed and focused on what I'd just learned. "How was the money taken from them by email?" I knew it was a basic question that could give me away, but if the woman on the other end of the line answered it, I was certain it would give me the best idea of what had happened.

"It's actually rather sophisticated," she continued, suddenly sounding animated. I sensed that this was the reason she enjoyed her job. There was probably a part of her that even admired the work of these criminals and appreciated the planning and the art of the con. Of course, she was on the side of the morally good, choosing to weed out perpetrators rather than being one of them herself, but I knew there was still that admiration in there somewhere.

"It's not the same as getting an email from a Nigerian prince who wants to give you millions of US dollars - and all you have to do is send over your bank details, or a little downpayment, to prove that you're trustworthy. The scam in this instance is more sophisticated and relies on timing and attacking an organisation rather than an individual. Having said that, it's often an individual who makes the fatal mistake. Essentially, an official looking payment request is sent with all of the correct information, and sometimes even relevant details about precise projects the money is intended for. The unwitting recipient thinks that this is the completion of a project and they need to fill out the details and return it, potentially even believing that they are sending it to other members of their own council. Spoof email addresses are easy to make. With just a little research, those ridiculously implausible scams you see on the internet that land in everyone's inbox become very believable. As soon as someone shares just a little correct information at the right time, well... it's amazing how often these things work. It's not so much due to the foolishness of the people who are taken in, but the timing and circumstances surrounding it. Plus, with anonymity of the internet and bank accounts that

can also be digitally manipulated and faked, it's pretty difficult to catch the scammers, but… that's my job! Clawing back
lost funds for the EU."

"I see how challenging that must be," I said, making sure I
affirmed and empathised with the woman on the other end
of the line, using every trick in the book to get her to keep
confiding in me and ignore any misgivings she might be
having. Misgivings like the person purporting to be a
national security agent having a voice that wavered up and
down an octave whenever the speaker got a little bit of a
tickle in her throat.

"All it takes is a momentary lapse of attention at the crit-
ical point and the money's gone," I concluded, wondering
which project the money had been taken from.

"How does this fraud case tie in with a murder? As far as
the file is concerned, nothing's progressed since the incident
was first reported by the mayor, Gabriel Sevres. I actually
thought the town was going to do some investigating themselves - especially when that reporter called on behalf of the
mayor's press team so the local paper could put out a factu-
ally correct press release about the matter," the woman on
the other end of the line said.

I felt my breath catch in my throat for a second.

"Do you recall the name of the reporter? I'm just trying to
keep track of every contact there's been," I clarified as soon
as I asked the question, not wanting to arouse any suspicion.
Although, if calling up pretending to be a reporter was all it
took to find out everything that I now knew, I shouldn't have
tried so hard with my cover story.

"Let me see… he left contact details in case there were
any breakthroughs. He said his name was Jamie Bernard."

I bit my tongue hard enough to let out an involuntary
squeak of pain.

"Sorry, what was that?" the woman asked, obviously

struggling to match up the pitch of the squeak with my falsely lowered voice.

"Just a… rubber chicken," I said, before wondering why on earth a national security agent would be conducting a conversation with a rubber chicken in squeaking distance.

"I see," she replied, not seeming to think it was a particularly strange thing to say. I'd definitely over-egged this pudding. "Was there anything else you wanted to know, Monsieur Martin?"

"No… thank you for your help. I'll be in touch if I need any more information," I finished, before saying goodbye and wondering if there would be any repercussions from this conversation.

My best guess was that I'd got away with it.

If Jamie Bernard had already called up pretending to be a reporter and had got the same information with relative ease, I shouldn't have been so worried. I'd made the assumption that whomever spoke to me about a fraud case wouldn't confide the details in anyone who picked up the phone, but perhaps these things were supposed to be a matter of public record.

And the question I should really be asking was why this wasn't publicly known.

Jamie Bernard had been tipped off by something which had led to him finding out about a massive fraud that had befallen the town council - a fraud that, even now, was being kept under wraps. I had several questions running through my brain at once, but the most important three were: How had Jamie found out about the fraud in the first place? Who else knew about the lost 100K? And most importantly of all… had Jamie Bernard been murdered to keep him from telling anyone else about what he'd found out?

I sat down in an armchair and looked at Spice, who was being a couch potato after the early morning walk we'd taken prior to the phone call I'd just made. "The secretary and the mayor know... but is there anyone else?" I said to the dog, who tilted his head and looked thoughtful. "I wonder what Jamie Bernard was trying to do with this information?"

A sudden memory of being told by Damien Rue that Jamie had even dared to bother the mayor at his own charity event flashed in my mind. "What are the chances that our murder victim was trying to blackmail two people in one night?" I mused, thinking of his other discussion with Sebastian Dubois that had nearly turned into violence. Perhaps Gabriel Sevres had been less reactive when confronted with a truth he'd been trying to conceal, but a politician would know that showing your hand immediately was the sign of a bad player. Confronting Gabriel on the night of the charity party could have been exactly the trigger needed to set events in motion that had ended in Jamie Bernard's death.

And the guilty party might just be the mayor of Sellenoise.

* * *

"Where are these signs of a break-in?" Marius asked when I answered the door to his knocking ten minutes later.

"That's a pretty good response time by most town's standards," I observed, greeting him with a smile.

"I came as quickly as I could. A break-in is a serious matter," he replied, puffing up with pride for a moment, before he noticed my expression. "There isn't a break-in, is there?"

"There was a break-in last night," I allowed, "but no, this conversation is not about that. It was actually sorted very amicably."

Marius did some rapid blinking. "Right... so..."

"I have news, and I didn't want your boss to be suspicious.

I thought it was quite a clever ruse," I said, thinking that Marius had clearly fallen for it, and he knew exactly what we were working on. I'd just have to hope that Monsieur Duval also lived with his head in the clouds.

"It was so clever that you didn't think to tell me it was a fake call out, so I've already logged it as a genuine complaint and will have the paperwork to fill out afterwards. You could have told me! Then I could have *pretended* that you'd asked me to come here for this reason," he grumbled, doing an excellent job of dwelling on entirely the wrong details.

"Tea?" I offered, hoping to smooth things over in the way I knew best.

"I don't drink on the job," Marius replied, clearly still peeved with me.

I resisted the urge to roll my eyes - which was never permissible as a therapist - and instead made my smile even more warm and welcoming. A positive attitude was always putting your best foot forward. "I found out something I think is probably important!" I said, overcompensating for Marius' bad mood and coming across as overenthusiastic.

Luckily, he was too sulky to even look at me strangely. "What is it? I have other important places to be..."

I ignored the fact that 'other important places' probably meant visiting the boulangerie to pick up Monsieur Duval's lunch and got straight to the point. "Jamie Bernard knew that the mayor lost 100,000 euros of money allocated to the town by the EU by falling for a scam in an email. I wouldn't be at all surprised, given what we know of Jamie's reputation, if he'd tried to use that information against the mayor and blackmail him in order to keep it hushed up."

Marius' mouth flapped for a couple of moments. "How much money was lost?! That's crazy! How can that happen? Those scam emails always look completely bogus. I knew it was a mistake having such a young mayor."

I raised my eyebrows. "I can see why Gabriel seems keen to keep this quiet," I observed after Marius' outburst, which surely would reflect the views of most residents. "Apparently, it's not the same as being sent something from a Nigerian prince. It's much more complex," I informed him with more than a little smugness in my voice.

"Oh, well that makes *all* the difference then!" Marius replied, not meaning it in the slightest.

My smugness vanished like all of the Maltesers sweets from a box of Celebrations at Christmas. "My point is, Jamie knew, and judging by the way we have a witness who saw him bothering the mayor on the night of the mayor's party, I think it's possible that the mayor may be more desperate to stay in office than is morally permissible."

"You mean you think he killed Jamie?"

"It's a definite possibility," I agreed, wondering if Marius was really moving as slowly as treacle this morning, or if I was being too vague.

"What do you know about the mayor's relationship with the deceased?"

Marius rubbed his chin, which looked like it had a smattering of stubble on it this morning. Judging by the circles beneath his eyes, he hadn't slept well last night and had likely risen late as a consequence. I was about to search for more clues as to the reason why he hadn't been able to catch a wink when I stopped myself. Marius and I were supposed to be investigating this case together. If I stuck my nose into his business, it could interfere with our professional relationship.

That was why I deliberately ignored the way his fingers twitched from the repetitive strain of holding a games console controller much too hard for too long.

Whoops.

"Let me see... in the mayoral race, Jamie Bernard did

run against Gabriel. There were other opponents repre-
senting the other three larger parties in the town, and even
a couple of independents." He noticed my raised eyebrows.
"For a small town, we have a lot of politics," he added, and I
didn't miss the eye roll that accompanied it. "Jamie was
never one of the favourites. You're probably not surprised
by that, but perhaps in his mind the race wasn't over.
Maybe he thought he could manipulate Gabriel into
somehow standing down as mayor and offering him up as a
replacement. He remained a member of the council, but I
know that meetings were never incredibly civil. That goes
for the majority of the council, so I can't say if there was a
personal grudge there. At least... not until this money issue
was uncovered by him," Marius amended at the last
moment.

"I wonder what really happened?" I murmured. Even
though the lady on the other end of the phone had been
helpful, the ins and outs of the events that had conspired to
bring about the loss of these significant funds was still an
unknown. When it came to solving a mystery, unknowns
were obstacles that blocked the truth from view. "We should
try to speak to the mayor and his secretary as soon as we
can."

A line appeared in Marius' forehead. "His secretary?"

"Yes... it was in her inbox that I spotted the email with
the acronym which led me to the organisation responsible
for investigating this kind of fraud." I considered for a
moment. "I still can't figure out how Jamie found out
about it."

"He probably did the same kind of snooping that you did.
As a member of the local council, getting access to the
mayor's or Selena's computer would be a breeze. People in
this town are generally very trusting. Having someone like
Jamie around was like putting a fox amongst chickens.

Gabriel and Selena really knew all of this and stayed quiet? Do you think they're the only two who are in on it?"

"We should go into this with an open mind, as always," I said, deciding to remain neutral.

I wasn't completely sure of Marius' relationship with the secretary in question. I hoped that - no matter what complicated ground may lie between them - he would remain professional. *Failing that, I will remain professional*, I told myself, trying not to think about the way I'd lied on the phone to a government official and was still locked in a secret war with Lucien Martin. I would be super professional... as soon as this all blew over.

"There's one thing I don't understand," Marius said, looking suddenly thoughtful. "If Jamie Bernard managed to find out about this money scam, why didn't he tell the whole town what he'd found out and become mayor that way? There was no real need to blackmail the mayor into getting him to step down. Jamie would have been a hero for finding and unveiling the truth, and the current mayor would have been ousted easily. It doesn't make any sense."

"Unless Jamie never really wanted to be mayor and was after a different kind of payoff. A more literal one," I said, thinking about the mayor's wife's clear love of fashion. Gabriel didn't dress like a rich man, but I suspected that was by choice and out of self-awareness. He'd been born here, and he fitted in, but I sensed he'd also done well for himself. That made him an excellent target for a man who seemed to have thought there were no limits to the things you could do to get cash from people - so long as it never involved actual work.

"That's probably it. There's no way Jamie could have handled the responsibility of being mayor. I think he only went for the position because of his ego," Marius agreed.

"I never seem to hear anything good about him," I

murmured, wondering if there were some who had a positive word to say about the deceased. In my experience, no one was ever truly bad to the bone. Good and evil was a sliding scale, and people landed all the way along it.

"I was going to come and see you anyway, by the way," Marius said, seeming to catch hold of a thread of thought that had eluded him up until now, after being floored by the announcement of so much money disappearing into thin air. "It's about the evidence from the crime scene... I thought they would have come back to collect it by now, but the gendarmes have left some of the stuff behind. It's still sitting in our evidence locker. And by evidence locker, I mean a broom cupboard where we usually keep lost property. It was only when I walked by the door and smelled something bad that I realised something was still in there. The mushrooms taken from the scene that were left scattered around the body have begun to rot, so they were definitely left behind."

"Why would the gendarmes not bother to collect all of the available evidence? Surely they'd do everything in their power to make sure that their case against Simon Dubois is watertight?"

Marius sighed and looked at me like I was a university graduate stepping into a job that, on paper I was qualified to do, but in reality was the equivalent of a toddler trying to understand rocket science. "They have their confession. The rest is unimportant to them. I didn't check to see if they've left absolutely everything behind. I just looked in and saw the remains of the mushrooms. Then, I slammed the door. How can such tiny little things smell so terrible when they go bad? It makes no sense."

Culinary complaints aside, I frowned at the possible implications of the gendarmes potentially neglecting the evidence. "I wouldn't have thought that was legal at all!" I mused and received another knowing look from Marius.

Justice on paper was one thing. The reality of the police system was quite another.

I shook my hair out, letting curls and the scent of strawberry shampoo surround me while I thought about our next step. "We should talk to the mayor and his secretary… and also find out what evidence has been left behind, just in case there's something important that was missed."

I thought back to the day that I'd found the body in the forest and everything I'd seen. I knew from past experience that, whilst my first impressions were usually reliable, a lot more could be learned if you had access to the evidence which had been extracted from the scene. Just about any key piece of evidence could have been concealed beneath a body that I hadn't been able to touch, and who knew what lay beneath the folds of clothing? Or if there'd even been something in plain sight that had been overlooked at the time, which would now become significant with new information in our arsenal. It was always worth a second look. Third and fourth looks, too, if you had the luxury of time and a willing police department.

I suspected this particular second look would involve a lack of time and a distinct absence of willing police departments.

Even with that foresight, Lucien Martin would have been delighted to learn I completely failed to predict the sticky situation I was about to fall into.

A STICKY SITUATION

"Justine! You are the exact person I wanted to see!" Marissa greeted me when I was trying to walk across the town square as inconspicuously as possible. This was proving to be a challenge for two reasons. The first was that I'd chosen to wear my usual all-pink outfit, and once again I felt like a flamingo amongst geese. The second was because I'd somehow forgotten that today was the day of the autumn fête, and every single person from Sellenoise had crammed into the town square. At first, I'd hoped that the presence of so many people would actually help to mask my subtle approach towards the alley by the police station where I'd agreed to meet Marius in five minutes time, but the inevitable had happened. I'd been recognised.

"It's lovely to see you, too, Marissa!" I answered, turning with the genuine smile already on my face. I loved seeing anyone who was happy to see me in return, but I did wish it had come at a time when I wasn't literally sweating at the thought of sneaking into an evidence locker. "What can I do for you?" I added, helplessly bound to my social nature.

"This year, I've been saddled with the dubious honour of

flogging raffle tickets. You can be my first victim. The grand prize is…"

My gaze was drawn by the dark figure who cut across the square with unlikely efficiency. If I was a flamingo amongst geese, Lucien Martin was a crow, or perhaps even a vulture, coming to pick at the remains of my fake psychic career.

"So, you'll take some, won't you?" Marissa finished, looking at me anxiously.

I cursed myself for tuning out what she'd been saying, but everything seemed to be remedied when I wordlessly handed over a ten euro note and received a clutch of tickets in return. "Good luck with it all!" I told her, flinging one last smile in my new friend's direction before I drifted into the crowd, following in the footsteps of the enemy who had been walking towards the place where I was due to meet Marius. I hoped I wouldn't come to regret not paying off Lucien Martin when I'd had the chance.

I stuffed the raffle tickets in my pocket and tried to make haste through the throng of people. Any other time, I would be pleased that the sea of locals didn't part the same way they had done for Lucien. Instead, many tried to engage me in conversation. It meant that people *wanted* me to be here. It meant that I might one day fit in.

Today, I breezed past in a cascade of 'Excuse me pleases' and 'Sorry, I'll be right backs', until I made it beyond the crushing centre of the square and into the less compacted edge, where people milled around, waiting for their chance to leap into the thick of it. I heard singing off to one side and glanced over at Julien Beaufort, who'd dressed up in an astonishing toadstool costume and was singing odes to mushrooms from the small stage he'd erected at his cafe. For once, his tables were packed, and the locals mostly watched with amusement, caught up in the festive spirit of the special day. It was a picture of local life and a heartwarming sign of a town who liked to come together to make moments and memories.

It was a shame that I was here to break their trust.

I gulped down the feeling of doing something wrong that stopped most people from sliding a pack of chewing gum into their pocket in a shop without paying for it. Now was the time to think of the greater good... and the greater good was stopping a miscarriage of justice.

The man they have in custody could still be guilty! a little voice whispered in my head, pointing out that the evidence could go either way. Without any sudden revelations, things remained as muddled as they'd ever been, but even if the gendarmes genuinely had the right man behind bars, there was no undeniable proof. And I was a person who liked proof... and pudding, for that matter.

I tiptoed around the side of the police station, feeling about as conspicuous as a banana in a lime factory. I half-expected to collide with Lucien Martin when I turned the corner, but Marius was the only one waiting in the weed-strewn alley.

He took one look at me and his expression soured. "Are you mad? I thought you'd wear something subtle! If you committed a crime, I could probably get sworn eye witness testimonies that you were acting suspiciously around the police station from 90% of the town."

"Well... it's a good thing I'm not a criminal then, isn't it?" I said, unable to come up with a better comeback. "Why are we meeting around the back of the police station?" I added before, with a horrible sense of inevitability, everything slid into place.

"It's like this..." Marius began, but I was way ahead of him.

"You're not seriously about to ask me to actually break-in to the police station and steal evidence, are you? I just said

I'm not a criminal! That wasn't me expressing a secret desire to become one. I'm not a rebel, I'm a fitter-in-er, just another sheep. I like rules! Baa!" I may have worked myself into a state over the idea of serious wrongdoing.

I'd imagined that there would be some rule breaking along the lines of sneaking into the police station to get a look inside the evidence locker, but entering any way that wasn't via the front door was definitely beyond my comfort zone.

Marius shot me a measured look. "As I was about to say, there's a complication in getting to the evidence locker. Monsieur Duval must have seen me open it the first time. He's removed the key to the door from the hook where it stays and is carrying it around with him wherever he goes."

"Wouldn't it be easier to put sleeping pills in his food?" I groused, thinking that it always worked in films.

Marius looked exasperated. "This is simple, and there's zero chance of being caught. I know for a fact that Monsieur Duval will spend the entire day of the fête by the wine stall. He's not even on duty, but he'll have put his uniform on for the occasion to extract free drinks from grateful town residents. I'm the one who gets saddled with everything on this day. Unless there's an easy opportunity for glory, in which case, he'll be only too happy to help."

"Is that why Lucien Martin's hanging around again - because Monsieur Duval has asked for extra hands today?" I asked, feeling relieved that there was an explanation for that vulture to be sticking his beak into things.

Marius' eyes widened. "Is he?! Where did you last see him?"

"So… that would be a 'no' then," I observed, the relief replaced by a spike of panic that we were walking into a trap. "He was going towards the police station. I haven't seen him since."

Marius bit his lip for a second, before making up his mind. "We have to be fast," he decided, rushing over to a window, pulling it open, and getting down on all fours on the ground.

I looked from him to the window in horror. "Why can't you be the one to do this?!"

"I'm supposed to be visible in the square! I'll be missed if I'm gone too long. It's a piece of cake. The outside lock on the window broke ages ago, the last time the locker was robbed. No one got around to replacing it. Just step on my back and jump through. You'll be in and out in no time!"

"What did they steal?" I asked, curious about past crimes in Sellenoise.

"It was a rare pack of *Pokemon* trading cards- stop stalling and get through the window!" Marius said, realising I was playing for time while trying to come up with another reasonable excuse as to why I wouldn't be going through the window. It shouldn't be hard to come up with something. Literally everything about this idea was bad.

"Now, look here, Marius..." I began, taking the fabled approach of drawing a line in the sand and then standing behind it, come hell or high-water.

"Monsieur Bisset? Are you around?" came the unmistakable voice of Lucien Martin from somewhere that sounded seconds away from him rounding the corner and discovering us dithering outside the open window of the evidence locker.

"Go!" Marius hissed.

For some strange reason that I would later agonise over, I didn't take the obvious route of escape around the rear of the police station and back into the square to live another criminal record free day. Instead, I galloped forwards like a mum chasing George Clooney, stepped on Marius' surprisingly sturdy back - at which point my senses returned to me, but it was too late to stop the momentum - and somersaulted through the open window with all the finesse of an Olympic gymnast.

Unlike an Olympic gymnast, I did not stick the landing.

There was a strange splat sound when I hit the floor like a starfish. I'd landed on something that wasn't concrete or linoleum.

"Ah, Marius, there you are! What are you doing? The pigs have escaped their pen in the square. They managed to free the goats at the same time, who in turn startled Madame Devereux. She fell on the geese pen and broke it, freeing ten angry geese. It's a war zone out there, but something tells me you're just the man for the job," Lucien said, arriving just outside the window.

I prayed that Marius had managed to get upright from the position he'd so recently placed himself in. All I could do was remain in my current pancake position and pray that Lucien didn't decide to take a look inside.

"I was… testing the window," Marius said, winning the prize for the worst excuse in all of history. "I thought it might have warped a bit in the cold weather we had recently. It's one of my duties… maintenance, I mean."

I scrunched my face up, wondering if his additions were making things worse or better.

Whatever was going on in the square must genuinely be every bit as dramatic as Lucien had made it sound, because he didn't ask questions. "Close it and come on then!"

"Right. Of course," Marius said with more than a little reluctance in his tone. I listened in resignation to the window sliding shut. The cold draught was immediately cut off, leaving me in a room that smelled stronger than a university student's socks.

"That could have been worse," I said, once I'd waited for the muted sound of footsteps to fade.

I peeled myself up off the floor and found it several times

stickier than was normal. "Then again, maybe it couldn't have been worse," I amended when I looked down at what had previously been a huge plastic pot of what appeared to be honey. It was now spread out dramatically across the floor, like a Tate Modern art installation. "Why on earth was there a vat of honey in here?!" I rhetorically asked the silent room.

Even though I was stickier than a partially sucked lollipop dropped under the sofa, I couldn't waste the opportunity to look at the evidence Marius claimed had been left to quite literally rot in the evidence locker. I followed my nose and soon found a blue plastic tray neatly labelled with 'Axe Murder 01', as if the person doing the filing had wanted to create a basic system, in case of any future axe murders in town.

I blinked and focused, putting aside my exasperation at Marius' ridiculous plan and my own foolish participation. "Let's get to work," I said aloud, lifting my sleeve to cover my nose as I leaned in closer, honey smearing across my face as I did so.

I tilted my head at the photos of the crime scene, left scattered on top of the other bagged items. I found a note in the box detailing that the murder weapon itself had been handed over to the gendarmes, which was something at least. Given the absence of investigative police work they'd done so far, I only hoped they wouldn't clean it off and hang it on the wall as a decoration.

Being careful not to touch the photos themselves with my fingertips, I picked them up by the edges, holding up each one in turn in the light of the window. Dust motes drifted between me and the shiny paper, and I was immediately transported back to the scene of the crime.

Everything was just as I remembered it. I felt my free hand flexing as I scoured the image for anything else, miming the action that would have led to Jamie Bernard's death. An attack from behind meant he'd probably been distracted, or perhaps he hadn't even seen his killer at all when they'd crept up behind him. I swung my right arm up and down in an arc, wondering if the killer had been there to settle a dispute over a mushroom spot, thwart planned blackmail over defrauded funds, or for a different reason all together.

I was glad the mushrooms were inside a plastic bag, even though it hadn't done anything to keep the smell inside. They'd been left on top of all the remaining evidence and the mess would have been unimaginable if the discoloured blobs of gelatinous goo they'd become had been allowed to run everywhere. Poking past the mushrooms, I decided that I couldn't see anything that had been catalogued which I hadn't noticed when I'd come across the body in the forest. I looked back at the mushroom goop and frowned when something caught my attention.

"Huh!" I said, bending down to get a closer look without risking leaving fingerprints on anything. I squinted at the globs of once-upon-a-time mushrooms, my eyes catching up with what my brain was telling me - that something was *weird*. I saw it an instant later. Small pieces of plastic, far too solid and bright pink to be natural, were scattered in amongst the mushrooms... like they'd been embedded there all along and had only become visible when the organic matter had rotted.

I shut my eyes for a second when I realised what the pieces of plastic were.

We'd been focusing on the wrong person.

With the rush that came with sudden breakthroughs running through my veins, I returned to the window to make my escape from the room that had revealed answers that had been invisible on the day of the murder.

"Gosh, that's a bit stiff!" I muttered when my fingers failed to pry open the window that Marius had lifted so easily from the outside. I frowned and tried again, succeeding only in bruising my fingertips. So much for my forensically untraceable entry into the evidence locker. My crash-landing honey print had probably ended all hope of that before I'd even begun my search. I tried again. The window didn't budge.

I had a flash of inspiration and trotted over to the door to the room, hoping against hope that it could be opened from the inside. The empty keyhole and unyielding doorknob told me I was out of luck there, too.

I shut my eyes and was forced to accept the inevitable. Someone was going to catch me redhanded tampering with evidence. I'd broken in with the intention of solving a crime that no one else seemed to care about. Instead, I could be the reason why the murderer walked free.

I was sitting on the floor in the middle of a seriously sticky situation when the window slid open.

CARDS ON THE TABLE

"**N**ow, this is a turn up for the books!" Lucien Martin said, sticking his head and shoulders through the window and resting his elbows on the ledge. "Correct me if I'm wrong, but didn't you say something about *not* being a criminal? I have to know…" He grinned and I could tell he was trying to hold back a laugh "…why didn't you see this coming?"

I took the time to take a slow, deep breath - something I always told clients to do before saying the first thing that popped into their heads. The first thing was not always the best response. For example, I wanted to tell Lucien Martin to go back to whatever hole in the ground he'd popped out from and get his annoyingly well-crafted nose out of my business. Instead, I opted for my second, far more measured response. "I hope escaped geese bite you in unmentionable places… and may your croissants always be soggy!"

Perhaps I should have gone with the first option after all.

Lucien looked delighted. "Was that a *curse*? I didn't know you're also claiming to be able to curse people. This will be an exciting experiment. When should I expect to see the results?"

"Whenever I get five minutes to release some geese into your house and pay the patisserie to give you week-old croissants," I suggested.

Lucien seemed to consider this for several moments. "I suppose it would be fulfilled."

"I would never promise something I couldn't deliver," I replied, managing to somehow get the runaway train back on something resembling a track. "How about your little bags of fun? Do they usually serve their purpose?"

Lucien's eyes narrowed for a moment as the unspoken question passed between us. I was asking him if he truly believed in their 'magic', or if he relied on the belief of others for them to have any measurable effect... like giving the superstitious a good scare.

"You seem to be able to locate them with remarkable skill, so perhaps you can tell me?"

We both knew that wasn't an answer, but it was apparently all the answer I was getting.

"What do we do now?" I asked, knowing that the time for smug comments and insults was over. I'd been caught with my hand in a very dangerous cookie jar, and the man on the legal side of the window claimed he was a genuine member of a law enforcement agency and had every right to follow the judicial course of action. I didn't need to be psychic to know how much trouble I was in. The only way out of it would be to appeal to the better nature of a man who had been sent to this town to take me down and had just been handed his ticket back home and more.

I did not rate my chances.

"You can start by telling me why you decided to break-in to the evidence locker of a police station. Is this how you get your psychic visions? You take a sneak peek at what happens behind the scenes and draw revelations from it?" he asked.

I didn't bother to conceal my sigh. Lucien Martin was still fixated on the fake psychic allegations. "No, this isn't my usual modus operandi. I'm sure you won't believe it, but it's the first time I've knowingly broken the law. I wouldn't have done it if it had been anything other than a spur of the moment decision, but... I mean... it just felt like the right thing to do. That the universe told me to do," I said, backtracking and doing a full about turn when I remembered that it wasn't only *my* liberty and future on the line. This might be mostly Marius' fault, but I wasn't going to throw him to the wolves. Only one lamb needed to go to the slaughter today.

"So, this incident wouldn't have anything to do with you and Monsieur Bisset going behind the chief of police's back to investigate what happened to Jamie Bernard? It's a totally isolated incident where you wantonly committed a crime with an unclear motive?" Lucien tilted his head and looked questioning.

I didn't know if Lucien had completely figured us out from the start, or if even now he was coming up with the most likely explanation for the position he'd caught me in, and I was about to walk into a fresh trap, but like a delicious piece of shortbread, I crumbled. "You've already said you don't think Simon Dubois is the killer. Surely you must support someone actually doing something to make sure that justice is done?"

Lucien looked back at me, his expression unreadable. I felt beads of sweat form on the back of my neck. He was enjoying this.

"I am merely here to audit the municipal police department and carry out any privately employed business that might fortuitously coincide with that," he said - like the utter pain in the backside he was. "Said private business might have drawn my attention to the fact that a murder case is being investigated, in spite of strict instructions and protocol for it to be left with higher powers." This wasn't really getting any better. "In all honesty, I'm actually curious about whether you've found anything." He shrugged his shoulders and shot me a 'How about it?' look.

"We might have discovered a few things that potentially contradict the confession the gendarmes have," I said, realising that Lucien did have a weakness after all. He'd been bitten by the mystery bug, just like me. He wanted to know what had really happened to Jamie Bernard.

"What things?" Lucien asked, managing to make leaning through a slightly mouldy window look elegant and luxurious as he wriggled his fingers, making the snake tattoo on the back of his hand jump and writhe. I still didn't know how he'd got those past employment regulations, but perhaps there were perks to being a consultant, as opposed to a regular employee.

"Things that I might be persuaded to share in return for me ending up on the other side of this window."

Lucien Martin rubbed his chin, enjoying making me sweat. "It's a deal. I mean, if I want to press charges against you later, it won't exactly be hard to prove who broke into the evidence locker". He pointedly glanced at the me-sized print in the honey on the floor. Honey... whose presence in the evidence locker remained unexplained. "Still, if you can convince me it was all in pursuit of justice..."

"...you'll forget all about this and be a much better person for it?" I suggested, getting closer to the window and trying to work out the best approach to the significantly lower ground on the other side. In theory, that should make getting out easier than it had been to get in, but I didn't need to be psychic to foresee that the difference between the length of my legs and the distance to the ground did not go in my favour.

Lucien smiled and his teeth glinted in that shark-like way I'd observed the first time I'd seen him and thought *predator*. "I'll consider a reasonable settlement."

I managed not to roll my eyes, knowing that I was still swimming in dangerous waters with a shedload of evidence of the crime I'd just committed littered behind me and all over me. I glanced back down at the floor, wondering what could be done about the mess before Monsieur Duval inevitably opened the door to the evidence locker to find the source of the terrible rotting mushroom smell… or, alternatively, whenever the gendarmes realised that their case would crumble in front of a jury and started to look for evidence.

"I might even be persuaded to visit the evidence locker and do a spot of tidying up, if the price was right," Lucien added, apparently now capable of telepathy.

"How about we talk about it over a nice drink at *La Petite Grenouille?*" I suggested through gritted teeth, motioning for Lucien to move back and then half-straddling the windowsill. Something told me that bargaining from the wrong side of the glass may result in the window being closed and all bets being off. It was better to keep negotiations flowing.

"I do always appreciate being wined and dined," Lucien said with a smirk. This time, I couldn't keep the eye roll to myself. Why was it always the ones who prided themselves on uncovering fraudulent claims who invariably turned out to be crooked themselves?

"It might make your local fan club jealous," I batted back, trying to keep my voice light as I negotiated the difficult part of the window exit and hoped that Lucien would do me a favour by not watching.

"We both know I don't belong here," he said with a casual shrug, miraculously looking up at the empty blue sky and giving me an opportunity to execute the final, delicate manoeuvre that would see me through the window and neatly jumping down on the other side.

My foot caught halfway up the interior wall. Worse still, I'd begun a forward movement that could not be stopped when I'd tried to swing my other leg up.

"Don't help me or anything," I muttered, tasting grass and gritty earth from my inevitable crash-landing on the ground. After the morning I'd had, I was tempted to just stay lying there.

"As I was saying… I don't belong here. You seem to fit in brilliantly. This town is full of crackpots," Lucien said, running a hand through his dark hair and making certain it was still picture perfect.

I frowned at the implied meaning behind his words. "Are you not even the slightest bit interested in personally finding out the truth about what happened to Jamie Bernard? I bet you'd be great at it," I falsely flattered, summoning up the desire to push myself up off the ground and feeling my head spin when I did so.

"I think you'll get to the bottom of it without my help. After all, isn't that what you're good at?" He cocked his head at me.

"I used to think so," I muttered, thinking that this entire investigation had been a mess from start to finish. And with the newfound discovery I'd made in the mushrooms, it didn't look like things were going to get any neater or tidier.

"Well, I'd love to stand around and chat all day, but I should check how your co-conspirator is faring at rounding up an entire farmyard. It'll form part of his final report when I submit the review. He looked like he was struggling, but you've got to give him points for trying. Oh wait… that's right, I *don't* have to give him points for trying," Lucien finished with a smirk, making me hate him all over again.

"Can you not even pretend to be a decent person for five minutes?" I muttered.

He flashed me a bright smile. "I'm looking forward to our business meeting later. I'll think over my final offer. I can't wait to see how you get back across the square looking like that, and covered in confiscated honey, too. There's a funny story behind that honey, but I'm sure someone else will tell it to you. Perhaps the chief of police will do the honours if he sees you coated in it. Cheerio!" he finished, lifting a hand in a strange wave goodbye, before strolling back around the side of the building with his hands in his pockets, whistling a cheerful tune.

With a sigh, I resigned myself to taking the long way round. I turned to face the nearly impenetrable bushes behind the police station with an unknown destination on the other side of them. Dressed in clothing that was more appropriate for a day out in Paris, I waded into the rural French jungle.

WILD GOOSE CHASE

I t was a whole hour before I made it back to the autumn fête.

The long way round had involved fleeing from a guard dog (who'd seemed eager to land himself a promotion), an encounter with an astonishingly well hidden swamp, and several fights with hedgerows that always seemed to be the prickly variety and never something friendly and civilised, like copper beech or box.

I'd taken one look at my poor pink coat when I'd arrived home and had put it in the washing machine, even though it had been dry clean only. Time would tell if I ended up with something the size of a postage stamp at the end of the cycle, or if my pink coat would be more suited for use as a circus tent. I'd considered Googling 'removing honey from felt', but I'd known that would not be smart, should the eyes of the law turn my way. It was almost as bad as a crime writer's computer being confiscated.

"Where were you?" Marius hissed in my ear when he managed to not so subtly wind his way through the crowd towards me. If anyone was paying attention, they would certainly think we were in cahoots.

"I hit a snag," I hissed back, my eyes searching the crowd for anyone looking back at us. Fortunately, everyone seemed more engrossed in the horrifying and fascinating sight of an octogenarian holding a bow and arrow, the point of which appeared to be wavering between a deer made of straw and anyone unlucky enough to be standing in the twenty metres or so on either side.

"What kind of snag?" Marius asked just as Lucien walked across the square, parting the crowds before him and throwing us a jolly salute.

My silence seemed to answer Marius' question perfectly.

"We're done for," he said, his voice rising several octaves.

I sighed, but I couldn't let Marius stew and worry over something that Lucien Martin frankly didn't care about. "He said he'd accept a bribe to forget about everything. It will be fine," I said, secretly hoping that Lucien Martin had a good idea of what a fair deal meant. If not, well... I knew an excellent mushroom spot for a murder.

"You tried to bribe him?" Marius spluttered, looking like he might be on the cusp of flinging himself in front of the arrow the wobbly archer was about to let fly.

"I certainly didn't suggest it," I replied, but I knew now wasn't the time to get into the reasons why Lucien and I had a complicated relationship. "I found something interesting in the evidence that I need to talk to you about," I carried on in a much lower voice, cognisant of listening ears, in spite of the hum of background noise.

"I think we might struggle to speak to the mayor today," Marius said, already making assumptions about the evidence I'd found.

"I think we can start with someone closer to him," I replied, looking in the direction of the mayor's secretary, who was tentatively nibbling a plastic plateful of sausage and what looked like potato shaped into balls.

"What did you find?" Marius asked, instantly sobering up when I heavily hinted that Selena was involved. I filled him in and his expression got even darker. "And I thought being outrun by three geese in front of the entire town would be the low point of today. Let's get this over with," he said, pulling up his trousers like a man heading into battle.

I grabbed his arm. "We need to be subtle!" I stage-whispered, or rather - pleaded - looking around at the crowds of people.

"Subtle... sure," he said, making an irate beeline for Selena, as if she'd bumped off Jamie Bernard just to annoy Marius. I was left to trail behind him, praying that the arrow that had just skewered Julien Beaufort's toadstool costume would be enough to distract the gossips from the obvious actions of my police partner.

"You're coming with me right now," Marius said, grabbing Selena's unresisting arm and frogmarching her across to the open door of the mairie. I allowed myself one final grimace before I trotted after them, wondering if Marius knew he was his own worst enemy when it came to keeping his job.

"Marius!" I protested when he and the secretary arrived at the mayor's office. He took her inside before finally releasing her arm.

"What's going on?" Selena asked, looking like she wasn't that annoyed with Marius and more annoyed that I'd come with them. I observed that she'd kept hold of her plate, which at least showed she had some of her priorities in order.

"We've got evidence that suggests you were at the scene of Jamie Bernard's murder," Marius said. I threw my head back in exasperation. In my experience, jumping straight in with accusations in the hope of getting a confession usually had the opposite effect.

"What evidence?" the secretary replied, putting her plate down on her desk and crossing her arms defensively.

"Selena, we know about the 100,000 euros that was lost to fraud," I said, jumping in before Marius could tell her every single thing we knew for sure and expect her to just spit out the truth. Even if people wanted to tell the truth, being confronted with facts that were being used to make them look guilty was never a good way to build trust. Empathy and a lighter touch was needed to encourage someone to confide.

"I'm not sure what you mean..." she started to say, but her face had turned ashen, and when she looked at me, she knew that I wasn't bluffing. I'd been specific enough for her to realise that much. "It was an accident and all my fault. I made the error and then Gabriel was just trying to help..." she tried again, shaking her head. "He should have thrown me under the bus. I was the one who messed up. He didn't need to do it..."

"Killing Jamie Bernard, you mean?" Marius jumped back in at exactly the wrong moment. Right now, I was tempted to use the roll of parcel tape that had been left on the desk to tape his mouth shut.

Selena looked shocked again. "No, of course not! Gabriel would never do something like that. I'm sure of it," she added, as if trying to convince herself of the same thing. "He was just protecting me."

"I understand why you decided to keep the monetary loss quiet in the hopes that it could be rectified before it ever had to be made public. I have no doubt that, given time, you would have released the truth to the town," I said, trying to repair the damage that Marius had done to this conversation.

"Of course we were going to tell people! We just thought

it could be fixed." She wrung her hands. "I suppose looking at it now, we've probably waited too long. It should have come out sooner, but it seemed like they were going to find the people responsible, and then everything would have been okay and we'd have explained what had happened anyway! We just wanted a chance to get the money back before people made knee-jerk reactions and the real problem inevitably became a sideshow to local politics. If only people understood that…"

"People like Jamie Bernard?" I said, working my way closer towards the truth of what had happened the night of the charity event. It was something that had ended in a man being dead with an axe in his back. "We know he found out about the fraud," I added.

Selena massaged her temples and looked tired. "That man! I swear…" She cleared her throat, seeming to remember that she was speaking ill of the dead. "Somehow, he managed to get his slimy paws on some information. I don't know how he did it, but he was always slinking around the place and never missed an opportunity to try to get one over the mayor. Odious man! He approached Gabriel at the charity event and told him he was going to tell the town the truth unless he was paid off." She shook her head with thinly veiled fury. "Gabriel spoke to me about it afterwards and said how worried he was. Jamie went off with Maia when she came over to see what the fuss was, and he was in a complete panic that Jamie would open his horrible little mouth and tell her something."

"Does anyone else know about the missing money?" I asked, wanting to be sure who was aware of the fraud and who remained in the dark.

Selena shook her head. "No, it was just me and Gabriel. And then Jamie," she added, her expression souring again.

"Do you know if Gabriel agreed to pay the blackmail fee?" I enquired.

"Of course not! He was unhappy about Jamie threatening to reveal everything, but bending to the will of a blackmailer is not something Gabriel would ever do. He prides himself on being an honest politician in a swamp full of liars."

I raised my eyebrows at that interesting description and missed my chance to tread on Marius' foot before he spoke again.

"If he didn't do the will of blackmailers, he must have had a more permanent solution in mind," he suggested in such a way that it seemed flippant.

"He didn't. At least, not to my knowledge," Selena replied, apparently taking Marius' words seriously. "Gabriel was smart. He told me that he'd pretended to agree to pay whatever vast fee it was that Jamie wanted to ensure his silence, only... he needed a few days to get it together. I think they met a couple of times after that and Gabriel kept saying he needed more time and that Jamie could add interest to the figure and he'd pay even more... he just needed time to get the cash together without Maia knowing."

The slightest of smiles appeared on her lips. "All things considered, that was the best part of his plan. No one can deny that Maia doesn't watch things like a hawk, so it was pretty plausible that Gabriel could have been planning a covert way to get the money Jamie was asking for. In truth, he was never going to give him anything. We knew that a day would come when Jamie would realise the money wasn't coming and spill the beans, which is why we'd already planned press releases with that day in mind. We hoped to get ahead of him when the day came. We hoped even more that the scammers would be caught and the money returned, but..." She sighed, "...it's looking more and more like it's gone forever. It's sad that our beautiful forest won't have those EU funded paths put in, complete with directions and named trails, but I'm not sure the locals were truly behind the project anyway. The forest can be a dangerous place, but I think a lot of them like being able to navigate it having spent their whole lives here. It adds a touch of mysticism to daily life, don't you think? Having a big, dark, threatening forest on the edge of town."

"Very *Brothers Grimm*," I said without humour. "I suppose you would be someone who knows her way around the forest and might be able to find a location drawn on a rough map? For example... the location of a secret mushroom patch?"

Marius had shown me the letter that had been sent to the paper. The way that Sebastian had shared the secret mushroom spots had been fascinating. He'd drawn a spider's web of paths and trails with annotations about distances and which turn to take, with Xs marking the spots where he'd picked mushrooms his entire life. I was sure that other townspeople would have similar maps in their possession that led the way to their own spots.

Selena's expression unclouded in an instant. I realised I'd pushed for the answer too soon. I'd like to be able to blame Marius, but this one was on me. I'd been every bit as impatient.

"I thought you were asking if Gabriel had murdered Jamie?" she said, proving she'd been paying attention to the conversation. Too much attention, if truth be told.

"We found evidence that suggests you were present at the scene of the crime," Marius repeated, unable to keep from saying it any longer.

"What evidence do you have?" Selena asked again, looking back and forth between us.

I glared at Marius and he glared back at me. Whilst we wordlessly wrestled with what to reveal and what to keep back, Selena reached out with her left hand and picked up a pen from the desk, chewing the end nervously in a habit undoubtedly born out of her daily job.

"There were false nails embedded in the mushrooms that were scattered across Jamie Bernard's body," Marius announced, apparently deciding that I'd lost the wordless battle of wills.

"Your false nails, I believe," I added right when I saw Selena was about to question the origin of these nails.

"How? I haven't been out in the forest for ages, and I definitely didn't kill Jamie. I thought... I thought you were here about Gabriel," she confessed, looking shaken by the implications. "I've actually been wondering if he might have done something unwise. I know it's a horrible crime to have committed, but Jamie was good at pushing people to their limits. Gabriel worked so hard to be mayor of this town, and he's been making a difference around here! Things are going well. For this to have happened is just awful. Maybe he couldn't bear to let Jamie Bernard ruin all that he'd worked so hard for. He's a good man. You have to know that."

"Such a good man... that he tried to frame you for murder?" Marius said, surprising me by reaching the same conclusion that I was considering myself. The false nails may not have been there by accident.

"He would never do that," Selena said, but she was sounding less sure of herself by the second.

Marius looked grave. "If we go by the evidence, then you must have committed the murder yourself. You knew the location, convinced Jamie to meet you there, and lost some nails in the process. Selena Indre, I'm arresting..."

"Thank you for your time, Madame Indre. We'll talk to you again if Monsieur Bisset has any further questions," I said, grabbing hold of Marius and frogmarching him out of the office in much the same manner that he'd marched

Selena into it. I turned and smiled apologetically behind Marius' back, before shutting the door and hoping that Selena wouldn't immediately notify the entire town that, not only was Marius investigating a case he'd been expressly forbidden from looking into, he was also making false accusations.

"She did it! It all lines up! Why would you drag me out of there?!" Marius exploded the second we were back at the bottom of the stairs and standing in the entrance hall of the mairie.

"Because she can't have done it, Marius," I explained, exasperated by both his behaviour and myself for having rushed into a situation without thinking through the facts I already had in front of me. Facts I'd had in my possession ever since I'd met the secretary. "The blow with the axe was struck like this..." I demonstrated, swinging my arm up and down to show him. "You can tell from the entry angles of the wounds."

"So?!" Marius spluttered, having watched my demonstration and got no closer to seeing the problem.

To be fair, it had taken me far too long to see it myself. I'd needed Selena's nervous tic of chewing a pen to be reminded of what I'd already observed when we'd first met.

"I just showed you a right-handed attack. Selena is left-handed," I told him.

Marius stood like a solemn statue as the knowledge sunk in. Somehow, I knew I didn't have to explain to him that this murder had all of the hallmarks of a killing committed in anger. A stab in the back in revenge for a perceived betrayal. The theft of the axe clearly demonstrated that the murderer had planned their act, but the act itself had been passionate, shown by the multiple blows with the axe. A calculating killer might have managed one blow made with a hand that wasn't dominant, but multiple hits seemed more instinctive than considered. In other words, there was no way a left-hander would switch to their right hand just to get away with murder.

Especially when there'd been evidence specific to them left lying around at the crime scene.

"Then it must be Gabriel Sevres," Marius concluded. "Or perhaps they even did it together."

"It's a possibility," I allowed, thinking that the evidence would certainly support a theory along those lines. Psychologically speaking, Gabriel and Selena had a lot to lose. Getting rid of Jamie would have been more than just a weight off their minds, it would have been a weight off their wallets, too. "What we need is more evidence," I said, knowing that all we had was circumstantial at best. It was little more than a theory, and in all honesty, we needed a confession.

"Look," Marius said, his voice filled with sudden dread.

I turned and followed his gaze across the square to where the gendarme patrol car had just pulled up outside of the municipal police station.

"They must be back for the evidence," I said with no small amount of panic juddering through my body. Had Lucien cleaned up the mess I'd made, or were two gendarmes about to start asking why there was an exploded pot of honey in the evidence room?

But as soon as the words left my lips, I realised I was wrong about that being the only possible reason for their return to Sellenoise. The first gendarme out of the car walked around to the rear passenger door and opened it, allowing a dazed man onto the street to blink in the sunshine. The gendarmes had finally realised that their confession of murder was nothing more than a concoction. They were releasing their prime suspect.

Freedom for Simon Dubois meant something entirely else for us.

Our illicit investigation had just come to an end.

We'd run out of time to find the truth.

"Why was there honey in the evidence locker?" I asked, my worry over the evidence I'd left behind getting the better of me.

"The honey? There's a funny story behind that…"

I groaned, realising that I wasn't going to get a simple answer any time soon. "We should find a way to get the information we have to the gendarmes. Perhaps they'll be able to get a confession out of the mayor and his potential accomplice."

"Or perhaps they'll mess it up the same way they did when they took the easy option and plumped for Simon Dubois being the killer. They might even fail to solve it." His dark eyes met mine. "We can't leave this alone now. We can get the evidence we need. Once that's done, we'll hand it over to the gendarmes, and it will be like we never had anything to do with it. I don't know about you, but I want to see justice done, no matter what it takes. The idea of having someone who killed another person living among us in this town makes my skin crawl. If Gabriel really was a good person, he'd have come clean after the murder."

I sucked air in through my teeth while watching Monsieur Duval trotting across the square, scraping his thinning hair back and trying to look as though he hadn't spent the day loitering by the wine stall. "What are you suggesting?"

"I have a plan to get the proof we need and a confession. It should be a piece of cake," Marius replied.

"Just like it was a piece of cake breaking into the evidence locker?" I muttered, having heard him say that phrase before.

"Don't mess it up this time," came the unsympathetic reply.

"I hope someone filmed your wild goose chase!" I bit back.

Marius just looked at me. "Meet me at midnight tonight outside Gabriel Sevres' house. I'll send you the address. And for goodness' sake, do not wear pink!"

18

ENTERING AND BREAKING

The house was dark and unfamiliar.

I forced myself to take a deep breath and then two more straight after it, keeping them silent, but slow. Normally, my pulse would slow along with my breath. Tonight it jumped in my ears, audible and unpleasant.

I shivered in the thin velour of the only black outfit I possessed that wasn't a smart dress for a funeral. The Halloween black cat costume that had never actually seen the light of day and had been bought on a flight of fancy wasn't a great improvement on brocade and satin, but I'd decided it was at least a little more practical for tonight's plans.

And what was better than wearing a cat costume when tonight I was playing to role of cat burglar?

"You're not here to steal anything. This is different," I muttered in the darkness, holding my breath for several seconds while I listened to the house. It was silent. I hoped that meant I was alone.

Marius had assured me that he had it on good authority that the mayor was playing cards with friends and would be until the early hours of the morning, as money changed hands and alcohol was consumed. His wife, Maia, was also out of town, supposedly on a shopping trip with female friends. When I'd asked Marius how he knew all of this, he'd just shrugged and reminded me that in a town like Sellenoise, everyone knew each other's business. It made it even more remarkable that someone had managed to successfully hide a secret.

Feeling a lot more certain that I wasn't going to be disturbed (whilst trying to tell myself that because no one locked their doors around here, it wasn't really breaking and entering) I took off my backpack and pulled out the video-camera that Marius had borrowed from a friend, who apparently had lots of them. I hadn't asked what he used them for.

I thought dark thoughts about Marius and his lousy excuses whilst I hunted around the kitchen for a good spot to hide a camera that was actually alarmingly subtle. I probably *should* ask for the identity of Marius' friend when this was over, just to be safe. The camera had the capacity to stream live to a computer, which was how Marius planned to catch the mayor out by recording a guilty confession - and perhaps even a visual - before anonymously forwarding the footage to the gendarmes, essentially gifting them the solved case on a plate. I'd been on board with that much... until Marius had told me that I would be the one actually doing all the hard work.

Just in case something went wrong, Marius was ready to bust in and wave his gun around shouting whatever came into his head in order to create a distraction that I could use to escape. He would then claim he'd been investigating a report of an incident, and we would all get away with it. If I got into trouble, all I needed to do was use the walkie-talkie I'd been equipped with.

How I'd be able to use a walkie-talkie if I found myself in trouble had not been discussed.

I'd queried why I couldn't be the one who got to run in with the gun, but apparently it wasn't believable and I wouldn't be taken seriously. With Marius' self-important words still ringing in my ears, I decided upon a kitchen shelf filled with dust-covered ornaments and reached up to place the camera there.

I squeaked when someone grabbed my ankle.

The camera fell out of my hands and shattered on the tiled floor with a dramatic bang.

"Correct me if I'm wrong, but I don't think you saw that coming either. You're a fake!" Lucien Martin said from his place hiding under the kitchen table.

"Why are you here?!" I said, blood draining from my face. Strangely, relief flooded through me at the same time, because it was Lucien and not the property owner come back to catch me in the act of setting up surveillance in his home, like a budget spy. Or worse... like a creep. I'd be kicked out of Sellenoise before I even found my feet here.

"I'm here to catch you doing something criminal. And it looks like I did!" Lucien lifted his hand and I saw a small camera of his own sitting there. "Smile for the camera, Justine French. You've been caught faking."

"Are you serious?" I said, my fright turning to fury in a second. "You've broken into a house and then lain in wait for me to break-in to a house, so you can catch me out and call me a faker. You seem to think you're above the rules, but you are not, Lucien Martin. You're every bit as bad as the people you claim to catch!"

He stood up and made a big show of rubbing his chin. "But I'm working for the national security agency. Catching criminals is my job description, which means I'm definitely within my rights to catch you up to no good."

"Except for the fact that you were here first," I bit back, not willing to accept Lucien's twisted idea of how justice and law enforcement worked.

He shrugged and looked smug. I turned my gaze away in anger, trying to calm myself down... which was when I saw a yellow folder lying on the kitchen counter. I reached out and picked it up, opening it and finding it filled with photocopies. Photocopies of all of the letters that were being published in the local newspaper. "I wonder why Selena didn't mention this? She said the mayor sometimes takes the originals home to check through, not that he makes copies of everything!" I opened the folder and there it was right on top... a photocopy of the letter and hand drawn map from Sebastian Dubois, which revealed his family's closely guarded mushroom picking spots.

"Aren't you going to confess to all of your wrongdoings?" Lucien asked, keeping the camera firmly fixed on my face.

Something was bothering me, and it surprisingly wasn't the man currently trying to record my downfall. "Why would Jamie Bernard have accepted an invitation from his killer to go to a secret mushroom spot that he would have imagined that only the Dubois family and he knew about?" I mused out loud.

I tried to think it through and concluded that it would be incredibly suspicious if someone outside of that very narrow circle had arranged the meeting. I'd assumed it was the mayor who'd called for the private exchange to settle the blackmail payment he'd promised to the deceased, but if he'd mentioned the spot detailed in the letter, Jamie would have surely foreseen the potential for the secret location to be used to frame the Dubois family for a crime yet to be committed. Any person with their wits about them would have smelled a trap. For all his faults, I did think Jamie would have known a conspiracy when he'd come across one.

Mostly because he was rather good at setting them up himself.

I chewed my lip while I thought through the unlikely scenario and tried to come up with a solution. *Maybe he didn't give him the location by sharing directions. Maybe he did it a different way...* I thought, before wondering how that could have been done without mentioning what the spot was used for, or how it was known.

"Coordinates," I said, unsure why that was the answer my mind had supplied. It hadn't come from nowhere. I'd seen something... hadn't I?

"Are you ignoring me?!" Lucien said, trying to get the camera even closer to my face.

"Be quiet for a moment, will you? It's on the tip of my tongue," I replied, trying to focus. Where had I seen...

Oh, that was right.

"That's evidence. That's the evidence we need!" I said, realising it could be enough. It proved prior knowledge of a murder location, and all we needed to find was...

The click of a shotgun being loaded made my blood freeze.

"Stop what you're doing and turn around slowly," someone said in the darkness of the house. "There is a gun pointing in your direction, which happens to be brand new. I won it for being the best shot at the town fête today... so I wouldn't advise testing my aim."

"Gabriel, there is an explanation for this," I said, hoping that using his name would encourage familiarity and trust... even though I was standing in his kitchen without being invited. Using first names probably wasn't going to get me out of trouble this time, but perhaps there were other ways out of this mess. For example... I could blame it all on Lucien.

Just as predicted, the walkie-talkie was unreachable in my pocket.

By my side, Lucien cleared his throat. "Would now be a bad time to accuse him of murder?"

19

PSYCHED OUT

"**M**urder?!" the mayor said, lowering his gun and looking confused. "What murder? I'm not really going to shoot you. That's not how things work around here. I just need an explanation and I'm sure we can sort things out together. There's probably a misunderstanding."

"There definitely is," I piped up, but Lucien hadn't finished getting us into trouble.

"The reason Justine is here tonight is to attempt to gather evidence proving that you murdered Jamie Bernard," he continued, stepping around the kitchen table and pacing up and down like a detective about to do a big reveal.

"It all began when your secretary, Selena Indre, fell victim to an email scam. 100,000 euros of EU funding was lost in an instant, leaving you and Selena scrambling to solve the problem before the truth got out and your political career was ruined," he began.

I frowned when Lucien paused to flash a smile at the camera he was still holding in his hand. Had the fraud investigators from OLAF called up Lucien when they'd checked up to see if he'd made the call to enquire about the Sellenoise fraud case? Had they filled him in on everything?

"I should have come clean sooner about the money," Gabriel admitted, dropping the gun barrel to his side. "It has gone on too long. I've been foolishly hoping that the scammers will be found and then all could be forgiven, but I don't think there will be a favourable outcome. I'm going to have to tell the truth and let my political opponents tear me to shreds, both for allowing the money to slip through my fingers and for concealing what happened. I deserve to be kicked out as mayor."

"But losing money wasn't your only crime," Lucien continued, still pacing and looking knowledgeable. I crossed my arms, wondering what *Miss Marple* was planning to reveal next. "You tricked Jamie Bernard into rendezvousing with you in the forest... at one of the Dubois family's secret mushroom patches that you read about in an anonymous letter sent to the local newspaper, which was passed on to you. Luring him there with the promise of paying for his silence over the fraud he'd uncovered and was threatening to reveal, you struck him down with a weapon you'd stolen on the very night that Jamie revealed that he knew about the fraud and was going to make you pay for his silence. But you never intended to pay Jamie Bernard at all..."

"You're right about that!" Gabriel agreed heartily. A line creased between his eyebrows as he tried to follow Lucien's explanation. I was mightily interested in where this was going myself.

"Instead, when he arrived in the forest clearing, you were waiting with Damien Rue's Bronze Age axe. Using this ancient weapon, you furiously hacked Jamie to death, striking his back in revenge for his attempt to betray you to the town. Then, your accomplice scattered mushrooms to complete the picture that this wasn't about a money scam...

it was about mushroom sniping. Only, Selena Indre made one big mistake. Fake nails are not good for practical work, like picking mushrooms. When she scattered them over the corpse, several of her nails were dislodged inside the mushrooms themselves. It was only when the mushrooms rotted that they revealed their secret... and in the process, they revealed the killer and his partner in crime. And before you try to blame your secretary the same way you tried to frame an innocent mushroom seller, the axe attack was committed by a right-hander. Madame Indre's dominant hand is her left."

"What the heck was that?!" I said, glaring at Lucien who was now leaning on the kitchen table, flashing winks at his camera. "How do you even know all of this?" I added. Only Marius, myself, and Selena had known about the false nails in the mushrooms, and the left-handed observation was something I'd only made in Marius' presence. There'd been no one else standing nearby, and I was certain Lucien hadn't been hiding behind a plant pot in the entrance hall of the mairie. I also didn't think Marius had suddenly become best friends with Lucien and spilled the beans.

Which meant...

"Did you bug Marius?!" I spluttered, realising that - while I was an expert at figuring out when Lucien had slipped unpleasant presents into my pockets, or hidden them in my house - Marius may not have been so alert. Lucien was an expert at sting operations. It made sense that he had access to electronic listening devices.

"I certainly did, fake psychic," Lucien said, making eye contact with his camera and raising an eyebrow at it, which would no doubt look like he was making a joke at my expense and sharing the humour with his legion of followers when the video arrived on the internet later. *If it arrives on the internet,* I amended, wondering if Gabriel would be amenable to lending me his first prize shotgun.

"By the way, you told Marius that you weren't psychic pretty much right after I decided to bug him when you two were looking chatty. I've had the evidence I needed all along. I just wanted to see if you'd stoop low enough to trying to bribe me into silence. And you did not disappoint!" He winked at the camera again.

"You forced me to agree!" I argued back, but if I were being truly honest, I shouldn't have let myself get into a situation where Lucien had been able to coerce me into agreeing to pay him off. Much like I shouldn't be in this situation right now.

Lucien tutted. "You're looking less psychic by the second."

"Who's psychic? Are you psychic?" Gabriel interrupted, whipping his head back and forth between us and asking me the question. "And what are you trying to say about Selena being involved with murder? She'd never do a thing like that! I wouldn't do a thing…"

"She's not psychic, as I have just proved on camera. This has been the exposé of Justine French, fake psychic, and you have been watching The Champion of Magic!" Lucien finished, pointing at the camera and smiling a Hollywood smile.

The banana I'd just taken from the fruit bowl on the counter bounced off his head.

"Hey! Now I have to do another take," he complained.

"Why would Jamie Bernard have willingly gone to a location that Gabriel and Selena were not supposed to know about? Did you think about that? It would have looked incredibly suspicious!" I said, asking him the same question I'd asked myself right before Gabriel had walked in and Lucien had proceeded to attempt to take credit for the painstaking investigation I'd conducted with Marius.

"What? I don't know. Maybe he didn't think it through," he replied with a shrug, rubbing his head where the banana had hit.

"Or maybe the location was given to him in such a way that he was intrigued by what might have been a strange coincidence," I said, thinking that something like that would have tickled Jamie Bernard, and I thought his killer had known it.

"Coordinates? What coordinates?" Lucien said, thinking back to my ah-ha moment and failing to take credit for this one because I hadn't yet given him the answer.

"Coordinates that were written in Gabriel Sevres' diary. I thought that they were postcodes, but I was wrong." I screwed up my face as I tried to remember. "463104 N and 17696 E. That's north and then east, just written without the usual spacing and symbols. When you put them together, they form a point on a map, and I'd bet you a bar of chocolate that it's the place where Jamie Bernard was killed. I'd also bet the phone number marked as 'B' that was written above the coordinates was probably Jamie's number. It was neatly done," I said, rubbing my chin for a moment as I considered Gabriel.

"Wait... *are* you psychic? How did you know that? Is it even true?" Lucien asked, looking unnerved.

I was sorely tempted to keep the lie going, but now was the time for the truth to come out, and that meant the whole truth for everyone present. "No, I saw it in Gabriel's diary on the day we first met. I'm good at noticing things," I told Lucien, accepting whatever fallout would undoubtedly come after this confession. At least I would no longer feel hounded by the lie I'd told. No one would be able to hold anything over me any more. It would finally be finished.

"So, that's how your scam works. You see things the normal way and solve the cases just using your powers of observation," Lucien summed up, shaking his head. "Absolutely despicable."

I threw my hands up in the air, silently wishing that there'd been a significantly spikier option in the fruit bowl that I could have flung at him.

"I did it!" Gabriel said, holding a hand up. "It was me. I murdered Jamie Bernard! Also, Selena had nothing at all to do with it. I took a set of her false nails with me in order to frame her when I picked those mushrooms and put them all over the man I killed with an axe. But it was all me."

Lucien looked at him and then back at me, his face splitting into a grin. "Perfect! Two birds with one stone. Man, this is going to look great when I post it to my channel!"

"You didn't kill Jamie Bernard," I said at the exact same moment as someone else.

The kitchen light turned on and I looked into the eyes of Maia Sevres.

"What are you doing here, my love? You're supposed to be having a good time with your girlfriends!" Gabriel said, desperately trying to get us to focus our attention back on him.

"I assume your wife is here to check if you're really out playing cards, or if you were somewhere else this evening. For example, you might have been having another weekly meeting with your secretary," I suggested, remembering Selena's calendar being marked with regular Thursday night briefings.

"It looks like I was right to come and check," Maia said, her eyes watchful. "What I didn't expect to find were two home invaders accusing my husband of a murder he didn't commit. I'd advise you both to leave immediately, and we will certainly be pressing charges."

"Maia is the one who murdered Jamie Bernard," I said, for

the benefit of Lucien, who was by now the only one present that hadn't worked out the truth.

"What? Gabriel was just confessing!" he replied, turning away from the camera for a second.

"It was the planting of the false nails that gave you away," I informed Maia, who seemed to freeze in place. "Fake nails don't fall off very easily. One might have been permissible in the mushrooms, but multiple nails? Selena would have noticed losing that many. Multiple nails being left in the mushrooms pointed to someone trying to frame another person for their crime, even after picking the location to frame yet another innocent party. I suppose it was sort of a double framing attempt. If one failed, the other would surely succeed," I said, doing some *Miss Marpleing* of my own.

"Gabriel's already said he framed Selena," Lucien complained.

"Why would he have done that?" I countered. "Why would he frame his secretary when he had already risked sacrificing his political career by keeping quiet about money that she had lost?"

"Hang on... what money?" Maia said, a frown etching itself in her forehead.

"There was an email scam. 100,000 euros of EU funding has gone missing, and I'm to blame," Gabriel told her, looking apologetic.

"Gabriel had no reason to frame the woman he'd been doing everything he could to protect from the wrath of the locals over what he knew to be an innocent mistake. He was hoping that the error could be corrected and the money returned. He had no motive at all to frame her by placing her false nails painted with her favourite shade of nail polish at the scene of a murder," I continued. "I think it's quite clear from Gabriel's character that he is far more likely to protect others than save his own skin. Even when sacrificing himself means justice won't be done."

"I said I did it!" Gabriel repeated, his voice level but his eyes imploring me to stay silent.

I couldn't let him do that. Not when he'd shown how selfless he was, even when he probably should have been a lot more self-serving. In fact, he could do with taking a small leaf from his wife's book, because no one was more self-serving than she was.

I looked at Maia and she looked right back.

"Fine. I did it," she said, finally making the right decision. "It wasn't Gabriel. I killed Jamie Bernard."

20

CAUGHT ON CAMERA

"You thought your husband was being unfaithful," I said, having seen the truth when I'd seen all of the signs pointing towards the mayor's potential for involvement, combined with the obvious attempt to frame Selena Indre. When I'd tried to match that with Gabriel's self-sacrifice for Selena over this money problem, it hadn't made sense. I'd wondered if I'd been wrong about everything, until I'd realised it wasn't the mayor who was guilty... but someone who had access to the same things that he did and also had a motive for both murder and framing the secretary.

"I knew he was having meetings with that woman and lying to me about it!" Maia said, shooting a furious look at her husband. "I gave him several chances to come clean, but when I checked up on his alibis, they either fell through or people were obviously lying for him. It was quite clearly a conspiracy against me! No one has ever made me feel accepted here." Now the furious look was in my direction. I decided to take it as a compliment. "It didn't take a genius to know what was going on. Especially when I dropped by the office multiple times and saw the Thursday night meetings written on little miss' calendar, as plain as day. I checked every week after that and they were always there, and yet, they never appeared in his diary." She shook her head. "I'd always trusted my husband, but it was obvious that he was hiding something. It was the only thing that made sense. That's what I thought, anyway," she admitted, looking chagrined.

"Jamie preyed on your suspicions, didn't he?" I said, knowing how the opportunist must have scented blood.

Maia brushed a stray strand of her luscious dark hair back behind her ear, returning her sleek, twisted bun to perfection. "I made the mistake of handing him that information on a plate. When I saw him bothering Gabriel at the charity event, I was certain that he already knew more sordid details than I did, so I accosted him, hoping to remove him from my husband and avoid arousing any further interest from other listening ears." She shook her head at the horror of people *talking*. "When I had him alone, I asked him exactly what he knew. I even offered to pay him for information, and that's when he fed me back the same line I'd given him... blackmailing me to keep him silent about the affair he said he knew my husband was having."

Her eyes widened at the memory. "It couldn't get out. It would ruin everything we'd worked so hard for! Gabriel's political enemies will stop at nothing to find a way to get rid of him. This moment of weakness was not going to be his downfall. I pretended to agree to Jamie's nasty little plan, but the more I thought about it, the more I knew I couldn't trust him. When I'd been willing to pay him for information, it would have been a one time transaction, but Jamie knew that Gabriel has money, and I knew how snakes like Jamie, who think of nothing but money, will never stop using anything they have on you, until you've been bled dry."

"That is a fair analysis of Jamie," Gabriel said mildly, still looking lovingly at his wife in such a way that broke my heart. I knew he would have taken the fall for this murder if we had let him.

"Why did you pick the secret mushroom location as the spot where you murdered Jamie?" I asked, still curious about that element of the mystery.

Maia blinked. "Oh, that. I was going through the folder that Gabriel brings home every week from work, just in case Jamie had broken his word and put a cryptic letter in there, or in case someone had said something nasty about Gabriel. I photocopy everything when it comes in to make sure I have time to go through it all. I'm actually the one who approves all of the letters for the newspaper. Gabriel is far too sweet and trusting. He doesn't always notice when someone's added a venomous sting to their words."

"This town is crazy," Lucien muttered.

"I found a strange letter that listed mushroom picking spots, of all things, and I suppose it inspired me. I was still trying to work out how I could get rid of Jamie Bernard for good, so I got a map out and found the first location the letter listed. I had no idea whether it was a secret mushroom picking spot, or completely bogus, but it was somewhere off the beaten track, and I also knew that Jamie was embroiled in various disputes relating to mushrooms." She tilted her head from side to side. "I thought that the thicker the smoke-screen, the harder it would be to see. I never actually intended to frame any mushroom picker in particular. I had no idea if the letter was anything more than a joke, or even who the spot 'belonged' to. I also had no idea who sent that letter to the paper in the first place. How could I have known? I simply found the location on the map and trans-lated it to coordinates. I had half an idea that Jamie himself was the one responsible for the letter, and had written it with malicious intent, so it seemed a fitting location for paying the first blackmail instalment. "

"You wrote them down in your husband's diary. You mentioned that you were the only one who seemed to use it," I recalled.

"But instead of paying him, you killed him," Lucien said, stating the blindingly obvious.

"Yes," Maia replied, looking at him with a light frown, clearly sharing my opinion. "He wasn't too keen when I suggested the trek out into the forest, but when I explained that I didn't want to be seen meeting with him in town, because I have a reputation to uphold and he's not the sort of person I would ever spend any time with, he warmed to the idea."

I silently noted that Jamie Bernard had finally underestimated one of his victims.

"What about the fake nails you took from Selena Indre's desk?" I asked, knowing that I was poking the hornet's nest.

Maia's eyes flashed with vindictive spirit. She may not have deliberately framed Simon Dubois and his son Sebastian - even though that had played nicely into her hands through coincidence and Jamie seemingly blackmailing half the town at once - but this had been a deliberate and nasty move. "I didn't think anyone would take it too seriously," she said, examining her own spotless cuticles. "I actually thought it would be the first thing found by whomever uncovered the body. I imagined it was obvious. Selena was supposed to be dragged in for questioning, and I'd use it as an excuse to persuade my husband to get rid of the interfering little witch." She smiled darkly.

"I would never have done anything to betray you," Gabriel said quietly, his warm eyes fixed on his wife with the same reverence I'd witnessed on the day I'd met him and Maia. "I didn't tell you about the lost money because I didn't want you to worry about losing all of this. I know you worked harder than anyone to get me into office. I hoped I could fix things without you having to fix them yourself, which I know you would have done. I... I didn't want to disappoint you," he finished, staring down at his shoes.

"And I thought that we were going to be ruined with an entirely different matter, courtesy of Jamie's big mouth. Either way, he would have got you," Maia decided with a single nod, as if it justified all that she had done, even if the motive had been a mistake. "Honestly, I'm glad I didn't know about the money. Unfaithfulness can be played off in public as a healthy carnal appetite, but falling for a money scam..." She sucked air in through her teeth, her mind more firmly fixed on politics and social reputations than the murder confession that still hung in the air.

"Please tell me you got all of that on camera?" I hissed at Lucien out of the side of my mouth, knowing that a woman like Maia would probably recant her confession as soon as she could. It was frankly astonishing that she'd been persuaded to share this much.

"No, I turned it off," he said, and I nearly hit him before he added: "Of course it's on! I live for drama. You think I'd miss something like that?"

It was then I realised that Maia was looking at Gabriel. I caught the question asked silently: *Would you do this for me?*

"Maia," Gabriel said, adjusting the grip on his gun. "Jamie Bernard was not a nice person, but there is never any justification for killing someone."

"I did it to protect you. Us. Everything we've built here," Maia said, her expression turning imploring.

"Sometimes, you can't protect everything that you love," Gabriel said, keeping his hand steady on the barrel of the gun whilst Lucien whipped out a pair of handcuffs, with all the panache of the glorified stage magician he truly was, and placed them on Maia's wrists. Her expression remained disbelieving, unable to comprehend that there were limits to what Gabriel would do for her. There were limits to what he would do to keep on ruling the society of Sellenoise.

There were limits to how far things should be taken.

"Here you go," Lucien said, pushing Maia towards the bush Marius had been lurking in when we exited the front door of the house together.

"What happened? What is this?" Marius asked, looking alarmed by Lucien's presence and annoyed by my incompetence - that had *obviously* led to me getting caught. When he saw that Maia was in handcuffs, his jaw dropped. "You mean that she…?"

"I'll get you caught up later," I said, thinking that, yet again, Marius had managed to miss all of the action. "I'll also teach you how to recognise an electronic bug," I added with a sidelong glare at Lucien.

"And I will send you the evidence you need to back up this arrest as soon as I get it off the camera and onto a laptop. In the meantime, you've already got enough puzzle pieces to hold her in custody. Call the gendarmes and tell them you caught the killer. Knock yourself out!" Lucien said as Marius moved to take hold of Maia's arm.

"Why would you help me?" the local policeman asked, shooting Lucien a look filled with suspicion.

Lucien smiled benevolently and shrugged. "You're a good policeman, Marius. You're wasted here, if truth be told. I think you deserve to take the credit for this one."

Marius hesitated for a moment, before he nodded and led Maia away to the car he'd parked nearby. His next destination would be the municipal police station and calling the gendarmes back into town.

I waited until he was out of earshot before I spoke. "You just didn't want to do the paperwork, did you?"

"I did not want to do the paperwork," Lucien confirmed.

"You really are despicable," I said with thinly veiled contempt.

"Perhaps, but at least I'm not obsessed with staying at the top of the game."

"Is that so?" I replied, not believing it for a second.

"Maia Sevres might have lost the crown in this town, but something tells me she'll love ruling over society in prison," he continued, ignoring my attempt to bait him.

I bit my tongue whilst I considered my next words. "You know... some people believe that they are always in the right and never in the wrong. It's an affliction, but it's one that often serves people well when it comes to succeeding in almost any venture. Some of the most successful business-people in the world suffer from it." I looked sideways at Lucien Martin. "The problem comes when you fall from grace. Take one step too far, and everyone you've ever trodden on when climbing the ladder to success is there to stab you in the back on your way back down."

Lucien considered. "That sounds like good advice... for someone who's just confessed to murder."

21

HOME

Lucien Martin knocked on my door at 8 o'clock the next morning. I knew the identity of the caller before I left the kitchen to answer the door, and Spice did, too. He tilted his rust and white head at me as if to say: 'Do you want me to bite this one?'

I only considered saying yes for a second.

Maybe two.

I'd guessed it was Lucien due to the hour being too early for anyone who cared a jot for things like breakfast and slow starts to the morning. It was also because I knew that a man like him couldn't let an advantage pass him by.

At least now it will be over and done with, I thought, feeling a sense of relief that Lucien Martin would be leaving my life for good, mixed with regret that the therapist in me hadn't seen him develop as a person during the time he'd spent in Sellenoise. I hadn't exactly been a saint, but I also hadn't fitted the mould Lucien Martin had been expecting, and I'd hoped that after last night, something decent in him would recognise that I wasn't a bad person. Today I would find out what my fate was, and whether I could afford to avoid it.

If that was even a real option.

"I'll let you know if I reconsider our no biting rule later," I told the dog, opening the door with a sunny smile on my face.

"So, you did it. You solved the mysterious case of the mushroom murder," Lucien drawled, leaning against the door frame.

"I'll be sure to write all about it in my mystery solving diary," I muttered, not at all amused by the way Lucien wanted to imply that I was a quaint little mystery solver who enjoyed sipping tea, eating cake, and crocheting in her spare time.

Actually, that was fairly accurate.

"Shouldn't we get to business?" I said, reluctant to invite him in - even though it pained me to keep from asking if he wanted a cup of tea, before feeling resentful for the rest of the time when he inevitably said no.

I was spared further deliberation on whether to let him in by Lucien walking right by me and into the living room. He immediately plumped himself down on the armchair, as if he owned the place. "I'll have a coffee with cream, if you have it. Black, if not," he announced, throwing me for a loop.

"Okay?" I scuttled off to the kitchen, unable to think of anything else to say in response to that. I'd already felt conflicted about not offering him a drink, and now he'd actually had to ask for one - the horror!

I checked myself.

This was Lucien Martin I was making the mistake of worrying about. He was almost certainly playing some kind of game.

I placed the filter and the coffee in the traditional filter coffee maker and turned it on to watch the slow drip-drip through. While I waited, I got out cups and a tray and even laid some biscuits on a plate, before wondering if he would think I was overcompensating for not offering him a drink.

"Sometimes, you're your own worst enemy," I informed myself.

"What a strange thing to be. I'm my own best friend," Lucien said from the door of the kitchen.

I frowned at the coffee maker, wondering if I was having an off day, or if Lucien was being particularly devious. At least I was certain about one thing: Lucien Martin was here to get something from me.

"What can I do for you?" I asked, managing to sound polite, in spite of the way I was seething inside at the hypocrisy - the audacity - of the man standing in the kitchen with me.

Lucien smiled and looked at the coffee machine, which was full enough to start serving. Apparently, I didn't have a choice about participating in this dance he'd choreographed.

"I thought that, all things considered, last night was a success," Lucien said when I'd carried the tray into the living room. He'd even helped himself to a biscuit, which was what I was currently worrying about. Was he messing with me by completely changing his demeanour?

A chilling thought occurred to me. What if he was in a good mood because he'd achieved his goal and had released all of the evidence he'd gathered against me during his time spent in Sellenoise?

I managed to wait until he'd drunk half of his cup of coffee, seeming to savour every sip, before I asked him what I could do for him again.

This time, he tilted his head at me. "You think I want money, don't you?" he relented.

"You told me you wanted money the last time we were in this situation."

"Did I?" Lucien rubbed his chin thoughtfully. "That

doesn't sound like something I would do. I don't think I ever mentioned *money*. I find that some things are worth far more. For example, owing someone a favour. It's amazing how useful having particular people owe me favours is. Favours are stronger than currency. What's better than having someone owe you something?"

"What sort of favour?" I asked, not liking how this felt a lot like an open-ended deal.

Lucien's smile spread wider still. "I'm not yet sure, but you've shown me you've got a useful skillset. I know that you're not psychic, but you still deliver on your promise to get the kind of results people want when they employ someone that they believe has supernatural abilities. I came here expecting you to be a standard con artist, but you're something much better than that. It could be useful to me in the future." He shrugged. "So... I'll keep everything I know about the mushroom murder mess to myself, and you will owe me a favour that I can call in, if, and when, I feel like it. Deal?"

My hands tightened around my cup of coffee. "I don't think I have a choice, do I?"

A smile danced on Lucien's lips. "Not unless you want to watch an interesting documentary about small town policing and the lengths a psychic will go to solve a mystery, including breaking into a police station to tamper with evidence, and breaking into a suspect's house to intimidate the guilty party into confessing to the murder. It would make very compelling viewing. In fact, maybe I'm being hasty here..."

"You know that what you've just said isn't strictly true!" I protested, well aware that I'd done everything with the very best intentions, if not with the most skilful execution.

"You're one of those poor people who is always trying to help others and do the right thing." He looked pityingly at me, clearly thinking I'd do better if I put myself first the way he definitely did. "The point is, I can make it *look* that way. It's the beauty of editing. The 'truth' can be left behind on the cutting room floor. I really am starting to rethink this deal. This could be my greatest exposé yet. I could even win awards. Not to mention the financial boost..."

"It's a deal," I said, knowing the methods Lucien was using to coerce me into this ridiculous open-ended agreement, but also failing to see an alternative.

The smile spread and became as toothy as a shark smiling at its lunch. "Excellent. I'd say something pithy about not changing your phone number or trying to flee, but I'm pretty good at finding people... even when they don't want to be found. I'll be in touch," he finished, looking at me with a kind of triumph in his eyes that made me seriously wonder what I'd just agreed to. Would it turn out to be worse than public ridicule, reputation loss, and potential prison time? It was hard to imagine, but something about Lucien Martin's smile made me think I might have made the wrong choice.

He placed his coffee cup down on the table, standing up and ruffling Spice's ears when he passed him on his way back to the door. He opened it while I hovered anxiously nearby. I'd expected him to walk out into the daylight and become a ghost, but he hesitated, turning and looking back at me. "You really are the best fake psychic I've met so far. Talent is talent. Don't waste it."

"You should be the first to take that advice."

Lucien Martin laughed and shook his head, as if I'd become the funniest comedian in the world. Then, he walked out of the stone cottage, down the road, and out of my life... until a day came when he would decide to call in that favour.

I hoped that day was a long time coming.

* * *

A lot changed in Sellenoise in the days and weeks that followed, and a lot didn't.

Maia Sevres was locked up for the murder of Jamie Bernard, and while a video taken during a sting operation by a consultant working for the national security agency was submitted as evidence, the handwriting in Gabriel Sevres' diary and phone records later established that Maia Sevres had been the one to arrange the fateful meeting in the forest where Jamie Bernard had met his end. With evidence stacked against her, she'd stood by her confession. No charges of breaking and entering were filed against any present on the night of the sting operation.

Gabriel Sevres came clean about the money mistake and the subsequent cover up and offered to step down as mayor in a snap town meeting held in the square. An impromptu vote was held and those present decided, almost unanimously, that Gabriel should retain his position as mayor and continue to work to rectify the error, instead of walking away from it.

I'd been pleased by the benevolence that the town had showed towards a man they had every right to be pretty ticked off with - more for the coverup than the crime itself. However, whilst I thought it demonstrated a tremendous amount of spirit, I was also convinced that his wife confessing to the murder of Jamie Bernard might have had more influence over the second chance he'd been given.

In the days that had followed her arrest, I'd lost count of the times I'd heard people whisper about Parisians always meaning trouble, and how it was important to look after your own because they were the only ones who could be trusted. Even though the mayor had proven exactly the opposite, that was the view they were holding onto, and that was why the mayor kept his position - through pity and a healthy dose of morbid curiosity. I hoped that Gabriel would answer their kindness by redoubling his efforts as mayor to help the community. Somehow, I didn't think I'd be disappointed.

The local gossips also had some interesting titbits to share on the topic of the murder itself. According to Marissa, after the gendarmes had come to cart away Maia, Lucien had called them back to the town and given them a thorough dressing down for their handling of the investigation and willingness to take the first easy answer that had fallen into their laps. He'd also criticised the way they hadn't bothered to properly collect or examine the evidence, and had cited their abandoning of evidence in the municipal police station's evidence locker. A locker that was in great need of a refurbishment, because - according to Lucien Martin - a wild animal had got in through a faulty window and had somehow spilled honey everywhere.

I'd felt a stab of relief when I'd heard that part of the story, coupled with a lack of surprise at 'a wild animal' being Lucien's idea of fulfilling his promise to clean up after my crash-landing. True to his claims that he'd genuinely been here in a professional capacity, he had also submitted his official review of the municipal police agents. Marius had been strutting around for a week when his police work had been highly commended. Apparently, the report had acknowledged that he'd gone 'above and beyond' when investigating local crime, and it had generously avoided stating that 'above and beyond' encompassed flagrant rule breaking and disobeying the orders of his chief of police when he'd been told to stop investigating a murder that was supposed to have been neatly wrapped up and tied with a bow.

Monsieur Duval had not fared so well.

The ins and outs of that part of the review had been kept under wraps by the man himself, but Marissa had whispered that there was talk of him retiring and putting Marius up for promotion, just as soon as another police agent could be recruited. I hoped for Marius' sake that he found a willing victim soon, and that he'd learned from Monsieur Duval's mistakes and wouldn't turn into the very monster he had always reviled. I thought he would do just fine... especially when he had a fake psychic on his side.

Lucien's surprisingly glowing report had meant that Marius had forgiven me for being unable to contact him when Maia had been confessing to murder. A full week had passed with him in such a sulk that, according to Marissa, minor parking infraction penalties had skyrocketed in Sellenoise. It was only when the review had arrived and news of Marius' personal success had miraculously spread to the local newspaper that he had finally shown his face at my front door. He'd then proceeded to tell me that he had decided that he understood the circumstances surrounding the midnight interception of Jamie Bernard's murderer and was willing to overlook the plan being improvised upon. He was therefore ready to return to the professional relationship we'd had prior to that fateful evening.

I'd told him to stop talking and had given him a hug.

We were friends, and we both knew it.

The anonymous letter revealing the locations of the best mushroom picking spots around was never published in the local newspaper, but what *was* released was a rumour about the source of Sebastian Dubois' sudden influx of money that had led to him being able to leave town and take a new job in the city. I hoped Sebastian was happy with the life he'd chosen for himself because I doubted his father would be handing him the keys to his mushroom business after he'd sold secrets to Jamie.

Simon Dubois had been welcomed back into the fold and liked to accompany selling takeaway cups of mushroom soup with stories about his time in incarceration for a duration which he made sound more like a year, as opposed to just a few days.

With Lucien Martin gone and the town's only outstanding mystery solved, I got to experience normal life in Sellenoise in all its charm. I even got my first client. After much tea drinking and talking together, that one client turned into three, when she referred her friends. Just a few weeks into being in business, my client base was already starting to build. Word spread that there was therapy available for those who wanted, or needed it, and so Sellenoise came, quelling my worries that Maia Sevres' actions would make the residents turn against all newcomers.

There was a seed of hope growing inside me which whispered that Sellenoise could be exactly where I fitted in. A place I could finally call home.

Little did I know, the seed that had sprung into existence when I'd first arrived in Sellenoise would burst into full bloom when Marissa knocked on my door on a sunny winter morning three weeks after I'd helped to catch a killer.

"I bring amazing news!" she said, dispensing with the usual greetings and jumping straight in.

"Tea?" I suggested, wondering if the great news could wait for something as important as a hot drink.

Marissa pulled an impatient face. "No, I can't wait. It's been hard enough keeping this quiet on my way here. I just have to tell you," she said, inviting herself in and giving Spice a hearty pat on the head as she passed. "I know it's taken ages to announce. It turned out that there were a few legal hoops to jump through before the draw could actually be made." She waved a hand and pulled a face. "The bureaucracy in this country could win awards for its pointlessness and ability to suck joy from everything! Anyway, it all worked out in the end. We pulled a ticket out of the hat, and... well, you'll never guess!" She looked at me expectantly.

"I'll never guess?" I repeated back to her, wondering what, exactly, I was supposed to be guessing.

"You won! You won the raffle you entered at the autumn fête. I am here to tell you that you are the proud owner of *Maison de Folie*," Marissa announced, as if I'd just won the lottery.

"I've won... a house?" I said, wondering if I was understanding her correctly. "You mean for a holiday?"

"Uh... no. You've won it. It's completely yours. That's why there was all of the legal fracas. The paperwork was slightly irregular. It happens a lot in these parts. There was a small matter of the building not exactly existing on the cadastral plan, but the darn thing has been there for several hundred years, so they can't very well tear it down now!" She cleared her throat. "I mean to say, it's a lovely old building in need of some minor updates. After a few tweaks, it will be a fantastic forever home for you! You can probably do most of the work yourself. You strike me as someone who enjoys a challenge."

"So, that was what the raffle was for," I murmured, remembering the clutch of tickets I'd abandoned in the key bowl when I'd been stripping off my honey-stricken coat. "I've won a house," I repeated, still coming up to speed.

"You have! So, now there's no reason why you can't stay here forever," Marissa said, as if reading my mind. "It's fate telling you that you are where you belong. I think you'll fit in here just fine."

And with words I'd been longing to hear my entire life echoing in my ears, I snapped on Spice's lead and the three of us walked up the hill to visit *Maison de Folie*, the grand prize in Sellenoise's autumn raffle.

I went to visit my new home.

A REVIEW IS WORTH ITS WEIGHT IN GOLD!

I really hope you enjoyed reading this story. I was wondering if you could spare a couple of moments to rate and review this book? As an indie author, one of the best ways you can help support my dream of being an author is to leave me a review on your favourite online book store, or even tell your friends.

Reviews help other readers, just like you, to take a chance on a new writer!

Thank you!
Myrtle Morse

ALSO BY MYRTLE MORSE

COURTSIDE CAFE MYSTERIES

Murder at Match Point

A Volley of Lies

Tennis Balls and a Body

Drop Shots and Disaster

Aces and Accidents

BOOKS BY MYRTLE MORSE WRITING AS RUBY LOREN:

THE WITCHES OF WORMWOOD MYSTERIES

Mandrake and a Murder

Vervain and a Victim

Feverfew and False Friends

Aconite and Accusations

Belladonna and a Body

Prequel: Hemlock and Hedge

MADIGAN AMOS ZOO MYSTERIES

Penguins and Mortal Peril

The Silence of the Snakes

Murder is a Monkey's Game

Lions and the Living Dead

The Peacock's Poison

A Memory for Murder

Whales and a Watery Grave

Chameleons and a Corpse

Foxes and Fatal Attraction

Monday's Murderer

Prequel: Parrots and Payback

DIANA FLOWERS FLORICULTURE MYSTERIES

Gardenias and a Grave Mistake

Delphiniums and Deception

Poinsettias and the Perfect Crime

Peonies and Poison

The Lord Beneath the Lupins

Prequel: The Florist and the Funeral

HOLLY WINTER MYSTERIES

Snowed in with Death

A Fatal Frost

Murder Beneath the Mistletoe

Winter's Last Victim

EMILY MANSION OLD HOUSE MYSTERIES

The Lavender of Larch Hall

The Leaves of Llewellyn Keep

The Snow of Severly Castle

The Frost of Friston Manor

The Heart of Heathley House

JANUARY CHEVALIER SUPERNATURAL MYSTERIES

Death's Dark Horse

Death's Hexed Hobnobs

Printed in Great Britain
by Amazon

26988838R00142